Retro Redneck Cult Nymphos Pound Sand

14 Explicit, Humorous, Related Erotic Short Stories
For Women And Other Prisoners

Vol 3

Purvis Carver

Retro Redneck Cult Nymphos Pound Sand

ℭHE PLAYERS...

Brandon Assman...Wily time traveler, killer, master of disguise, and now a federal agent. Capriciously murdered famous detective P.G. Pimperton.

Johnny Behen... A temperamental egoist who does as he pleases. Happy-go-lucky. An unhinged sex addict... Ballplayer and a former crooked sheriff. Suspected sex trafficker.

Charlie Mansion... Psychotic cult leader and manipulator of women.

Squeaky Clean... Shapely, fun-sized killer for Charlie.

Poison Penis-Envie...Twitchy brunette silent porno star turned sex therapist turned cult witch who can morph into Little Lil.

Lizzie Bordone... A chick Behen picks up at a funeral, who then vanishes in Reno.

Mike Nelson... Surly silent male porno star and scuba diver

Frank Savage... Stocky, swarthy Death Valley blowhard, hard-drinking gambler/pimp with a violent history and a remarkable record of scoring with beautiful women.

Norma Skinner... Amargosa prostitute, paramour to Frank Savage. Beautiful, hardened denizen of the red-light district.

Lecher Christian... Brooding Lothario...Time-traveling navy mutineer turned old west snake oil salesman and Navy sex trafficker.

Holly Payton... Follows Behen from Portland the South Gate. Kidnapped by Cobb and taken to Bodie. Now with Mr. Christian.

Albert Ball.... Crooked Interior Secretary before becoming Acting President. Puts the country under Sheria law after Hardening is shot.

Virginia Dickens... Trying to survive in Bodie after tragedy befalls her family.

Lloyd Sweety... Mild-tempered contemporary bank examiner turned time-traveling vicious killer in Old West Bodie.

Lawrence Lizard-Lounge... The artist formerly known in the twenty-first century as Larry Lounge-Lizard.

Maryann Pimperton-O'Henry... Mrs. Pimperton's daughter. Married to the missing sex trafficker.

Augie O'Henry... Reno sex trafficker linked to the Lake Tahoe murder. A rival sex trafficker to Cecil Fergoosen.

Helen Fergoosen... Reno Civil War prostitute who marries into the wealthy Fergoosen family.

Cecil Fergoosen... Patriarch of the family's real estate and sex trafficking empire in Nevada and eastern California. Married to Helen.

Walter Fergoosen...Secret service agent assigned to the president.

Darren Dreihole... St. Louis Browns pitcher who claims to be seeking the killer of his murdered father-in-law.

Mavis Dreihole... Darren's uptight wife can't hold a dick inside of her for more than a minute because of her lesbian tendencies.

Katie Davy...Professional perjurer, ex-prostitute, and silent porno actress who shows up in Las Vegas hawking hot air balloon trips.

Cappy... Mansion Family member who would never forgive herself for not killing her grandmother.

Sadie... Mansion Family murderer who would never forgive herself for getting caught.

Tex Hunter... Mansion family tough guy who goes on hallucinatory murder sprees at Charlie's behest over two nights outside of Los Angeles.

Sandi... Good-looking and deadly serious militia woman for Charlie.

Mother Mary... Plain-Jane, an original member of the Mansion family sex/murder cult.

Gypsy... Sexy, free-spirited cult member, articulate, a the top recruiter.

Lulu... Enjoyed every minute of time in the Family, especially the murder part.

Bobby... Silent porno star, musician, and killer under Charlie's control.

Slim --- Bi-polar psycho killer and overall, Mansion Family thug.

Paul... Hippie stoner who is part of Mansion Family.

Simi Valley... Cute Mansion chick. One of the newest cult members.

Linda Kastabian... A free-loving, smiling redheaded witch who copped a plea and ducked murder raps.

Piggy... Quiet Mexican girl and Linda's alter-ego. Proves that you can be in two places at one time if you're a witch.

Brenda Pitman… When's she's around, people die.

Antoinette… Baby daughter of the famous Hawaiian polygamist and botanist, Francisco de Paula marin.

Lyman Swale… Her swindler husband.

Jonah… Known as Cupid. The youngest of the three Hawaiian surfer dude brothers.

Koa… The eldest of the Hawaiian surfer dude brothers. A playboy and beach bum.

Edward… The littlest of the three Hawaiian surfer dude brothers. Frail and sickly.

Martin… The surfer dudes' charming cousin who already has 13 children by three wives.

Senator Robert Mendacious… Charged with bribery by Brandon Assman.

Orville Rickenbacker Wright… Unregulated early twentieth-century airplane pilot.

Gobby Smack… First Witch of Teenography. Brutally honest. brunette.

Quote Unquote… Second Witch of Teenography… Enthusiastic brunette with one foot in and the other out of the cult.

Furtha Ada0-Do…Third Witch of Teenography. A lesbianic tomboy blonde who looks like Dennis the Menace.

Blue Scout... Fourth Witch of Teenography... Blonde and infantile girlie girl.

Robite Tumbler... Perky Fifth Witch... Outgoing. All for the little man except when she's with the big man.

Linda Kastabian... Smiling redneck Brandon meets at the witches' coven. Later joins Mansion cult as Piggy.

Chief Liggy-gaga... Avidly awaiting the arrival of John Frum to the Island of Tanna in the South Pacific nation of Vanuatu.

Yaawa... Chief Liggy-gaga's daughter on the South Pacific Island of Tanna. Moves to California to become a witch.

Petuni... Yaawa's sister on Tanna.

Vevuk... Yaawa's lover on Tanna.

Abby Fine... Gentle and loving. The Sixth and Only Black Witch of Teenography.

Father Luis Cervantes... A horny priest who won't take no for an answer.

Sister Amelia... Former silent porno star. Now a devout nun.

Layla... Cheeky waitress at the Jungle Room

Motha Superior... Thick black woman who runs the Parrish.

Ned McLain… Spoiled rich kid. Former Washington Post editor and Harding's unofficial pimp.

Mary Ann Wells… Cute and vivacious young lady trapped in a gay cult at the Ponderosa.

Adam Cartwright… Her former boyfriend. Now residing in the lunatic asylum in Waco.

Ben Cartwright… Patriarch and cult leader at the Ponderosa.

Walter Fergoosen… Secret service agent and nephew to the murdered Cecil Fergoosen.

Miss Goodbody… Prim school teacher by day and red-hot sex worker by night who finds herself going back in time.

Penelope Hurst… George's patriotic and politically liberal wife who works as a comfort woman to support the troops.

Goober Cleveland… Fat, amorous walrus of a politician running for President on the Progressive Buggy Insurance Ticket.

Corporal Outman… Earnest soldier at Bitter Creek.

Major Patches… Battlefield commander at Bitter Creek.

Emily Showers… Cobb's sister. Curvaceous brunette married to the Mono County Sheriff and a freak at the masquerade ball.

***Jack Holmes*...** Serial killer Pamela and Sylvia met at the St. Louis World's Fair.

***June bug*...** Hot little Asian number who hangs out in Swinger's clubs.

***Allegra Kole*....** Brandi's feral friend.

***Pong Ping*...** Chubby and smiling crib prostitute, news anchor, and presidential assassin from Los Angeles.

***Carolyn Herringbone*...** Former school teacher colleague of Miss Priminger. Mannerly and uptight. Comfort woman and mistress to General McArthur.

***Nancy Priminger*...** Tall, sweet young schoolteacher who's kidnapped by the Kempeitai and sent to a comfort woman unit in Ventura.

***A. W. Clark*...** U.S. Senator and captain of industry with a dubious reputation.

***Chanel Clark*...** Second wife of Senator A.W. Clarke

***Roulette Clark*...** Quiet daughter of railroad and mining magnet, A.W. Smith.

***Mortimer G. Shyster Esquire*...** Brandon Assman's idea of the best attorney in Reno.

***Veronica*...** Intense silent porno star who likes to bang her head against the wall.

***Officer Falstein*...** No-nonsense Capitol police officer.

Madame Koolista...Spiritualist to Mrs. Harding. Later, a Supreme Court Justice.

Admiral Nimnutz... Cigar chomping Chief of Naval Operations under Acting President Ball.

Botched Robbery

According to what Sadie told me later, she, along with Mary and my handsome boyfriend, Bobby, rode out Topanga Canyon Road to confront Gary Hitman about the bad mescaline he had sold Charlie. The same Charlie Mansion who used to beat me when I would fall asleep during one of his crazy indoctrination rants.

They walked up the steep stairs from the road to Hitman's house which overhung the hillside, rapped on the door and Gary let them in. When confronted, Gary claimed there was nothing wrong with the drugs and refused to refund the money. Bobby began pistol-shipping Gary, who swore he couldn't return the money because it had already been spent. Bobby handed Sadie the gun and told her to keep it pointed at Gary while he searched the house. Sadie was to shoot Gary if he moved. Instead, Sadie set the gun on the table. When

Gary lunged for it, a scuffle ensued. Bobby rushed in, fought Gary for the gun, and gained possession of it.

Bobby told Mary to call Charley and report the problem. Charley got on the phone. He instructed Bobby to keep Gary covered and to wait for him and Bruce to get there.

… An hour later, Charley and Bruce Dorn, Charlie's right-hand man, came riding up. Charlie entered the house holding a samurai sword. He didn't take long to use it. Charlie sliced the side of Gary's face and nearly took off Gary's left ear.

"That's how to be a man," Charlie told Bobby. "Now don't leave here without settling the situation."

"But there's no money here," Bobby objected.

"The man just inherited $2,100 from his granny, a silent porno star in Chicago, so don't tell me there's no money here."

Bobby, a San Francisco silent porno actor, could identify with that, but I don't think he ever worked with Gary's granny… I hope not anyway.

After Charlie and Bruce left, Sadie recalled, she, Bobby, and Mary tortured Gary for three days. Gary kept whining about his ear, so Sadie and Mary tried to sew it back together with dental floss. I enjoy sewing too but have never had to sew an ear back on. That effort was less than satisfactory to Gary, who began clambering for a doctor.

Finally, a deal was struck. Gary agreed to give Bobby a signed Bill of Sale for his two horses. Bobby told Sadie and Mary to wipe the place down and the two women went to the kitchen to do that.

The more Gary asked for a doctor, the more paranoid Bobby became. Fearing that Gary would go to the police, Bobby went into the kitchen and told the women that he would have to kill Gary.

"Do what you have to do," Sadie replied.

Bobby went back to Gary and stabbed him twice in the chest. With the job completed, the three purple-traitors locked up the house, leaving Gary clutching his beads and chanting some Buddhist shit.

Halfway down the steps, Bobby paused. "We can't leave him like that," he said. Bobby climbed through the window and back into the house. When he came out, he said that he had smothered Gary with a pillow.

They took Gary's horses and rode to a nearby restaurant for a bite to eat.

Bobby told Sadie that he should have killed her for failing to pick up the gun.

The three split up after that with Sadie and Mary returning to the ranch to share their exciting story.

"What did you think about all that?" I asked.

Sadie laughed and in her clear, high-pitched voice, replied, "I didn't think anything about it, Liz."

"But you killed Gary."

"There's nothing wrong with killing a pig."

Just as I was starting to miss Bobby, who had been arrested, a mysterious stranger, who had almost died in the desert, appeared at the ranch. I helped nurse him back to health. All the other girls liked him. I liked him more. He had a swagger about him. We named him, Pal-Mal Man.

Charlie hated him.

KISSES ON THE RAINDROPS

After apprehending crooked Senator Mendacious and his lovely wife, Nadine, who offered to fuck me if I let her go, I headed west to Reno, Nevada to resume the search for the mysterious Augie O'Henry, a person of interest in the Cecil Fergoosen murder.

I met up with Fergoosen's nephew, Under the Covers agent... I mean, Secretive Service agent, Walter Fergoosen along with James West, was on duty the night President Hardening was murdered.

"Well, if it ain't Brandon Assman. Done any time-traveling lately?"

"Too busy for vacations." ... I asked Walter why he didn't step up that night and take a bullet for the president.

"What? Do you think I'm crazy?"

Walter informed me that Cecil's daughter, Mavis Dreihole, husband to Darren Dreihole, the hard-throwing St. Louis Browns left-hander, had moved back to Tahoe to care for her ailing mother, Helen Fergoosen, who was seriously injured in the attack. Furthermore, Mavis Dreihole's friend (and maybe more), Maryann O'Henry, had accompanied her. Mrs. O'Henry was who I wanted to interview again in respect to the whereabouts of her husband, Augie.

Arriving in Tahoe by train late Sunday night, I went to the Fergoosen home, which overlooked the lake, creepy-crawled through the window, and slipped into bed with Mrs. Dreihole and Mrs. O'Henry, both. They confirmed the rumor about the two women whose husbands had been friends until they weren't.

"Oh, Darrin. You're home!" Marvis said in the darkened room. "Was there a rainout?"

"No, I came in my pants," I replied in Darren's voice.

The candlestick phone rang. Maryann O'Henry answered it.

"Augie? Where are you? Are you alright?" … Well, it's hard… The grief I bear… No, I'm not taking cock just yet. Darren's on Mavis right now… Well, I can't just tell him to get off. She's his wife after all… Augie I want to see you… What did I just say? Would you mind? You're where?

Ballarat? Where's that? … Where in California? …Where's Barker Ranch? … North of Ballarat. Okay…"

I got on top of Mrs. O'Henry…

"Dick? … I know you're name is Augie… Oh, that feels good. Don't stop, Darren… Well, I can't just tell him to get off, Augie….Because Darren is the youngest of any player to do it… No, not pitch a no-hitter. Kill his father-in-law."

I couldn't believe Maryann would do that. Fuck my best friend, Darren Dreihole. I'm an innocent man, after all. So, what right does my lovely wife have to cheat on me?

"Augie O'Henry… Falsely accused of the Cecil Fergoosen murder."

"Huh?"

I turned around. This cute hippie girl was smiling at me. "Were you listening in on my conversation?"

"Reprieved when a train wreck freed him in route to the whorehouse…

"Freed him to hide in lonely desperation under the influence of heavy narcotics… To impersonate a French painter… a cheap detective… a silent porno movie star…

"Freed him to run before the relentless pursuit of Under the Covers special agent, Brandon Assman, an Old West detective obsessed with finding fresh pussy.

"Freed him to search for a man with a big dick he saw leave the scene of the crime. A man by the name of Danny Corlotto, a member of the Mansion family in Death Valley.

"... Death Valley. A desert inhabited by snakes, beetles, poisonous spiders, and—".

"Gonorrhea-infested hippie chicks like Steamy Valley... Come on."

"How did you know my name?"

Following a shitstorm like I hadn't experienced in weeks; I boarded the train back to Reno to deal with the shit going on in my life there.

Checking in at the Reno post office, I noticed a notice on the wall about a missing nine-year-old girl... Nothing in my mailbox, however. Nothing for Brandon Assman. That figured. Well, no news is good news, I suppose.

I booked a stagecoach passage to Las Vegas and then mingled with passengers at the depot hoping someone would say something stupid that would give me a big laugh.

I didn't have to wait long. This bearded little guy with a disturbingly toothless grin was showing off in front of his bitches. The names Gypsy, Squeaky, Sandi, Lulu, and Cappy popped out. I filed them away. The twitchy guy looked at me.

"What are you staring at, friend?"

"Aren't you Charlie Mansion?" His face went through a series of quick expression changes like it was a silent movie.

"Which one?" he laughed.

I recognized a couple of the personas he was trying out from his mug shot. "I see you're back to pimping."

"I don't mind what you say about me," Gypsy said, "but how dare you say that about Squeaky. She's lesbian."

"Sex Trafficking. Not pimping," Charley giggled. "I like them young,"

"What are you a fuckin' pig?" Squeaky asked. "Come to ruin my day and disposition?"

"That's not my style."

"All aboard!"

We scrunched into the stagecoach.

"I never receive mail on Mondays," I said as the stage sped south toward Las Vegas. "And I don't know why that is."

"I know why, Pal-Mal Man," Charlie responded. Everybody looked at him. "Because if you received mail on Mondays, they'd have to give you some more on Tuesdays and every other day of the week – feed the pig, dig? ... They have better things to do on Tuesday and on all of them other days like fuck British postal whores in the missionary position only...

"... Don't be such a pig, man... Mail on Monday. Whoever heard of such a stupid idea?"

"... Have heart failure with related symptoms?" Squeaky asked me.

"No, thank you. I don't want any," I replied. "What's up with the missing girl?"

"That ain't current," Charlie replied. "They found her,"

"She gets fucked?"

"War in Israel ain't news either. It happened yesterday. Why can't them lazy-ass establishment pig reporters go dig up some news. ... I'll give them some news... News derives from the word, new... War ain't new. It happened yesterday. Missing girl ain't *new*. That means it ain't *news* because they found her. Dig?"

"Not if I don't have to… She gets fucked?"

"The purple—traitor sent the parents a random note."

"You mean a ransom note?"

"Yeah, man.

"You fuck her, Charlie?"

"I refuse to answer, Pal-Mal Man, on the grounds it may tend to discriminate against me."

"You have a hot body," I told Squeaky. "Fun-sized. I'd like to screw my prick into it."

"Better hurry up before some other pig does."

"Pigs," Sandi said with contempt. "All they want to do is fuck."

Sandi was a good-looking, college-educated psycho who reminded me of a female version of Bodie town marshal, Ronny McKay,

Lulu said, "You should come to our place. We're staying at Angela Lansberry's house in the Hollywood Hills. It's nice… Got an outdoor pool, dungeon, billiard room… everything."

"How'd you meet her?"

Squeaky said, "She gave us a ride in her carriage. Nice lady."

Gypsy reminded her, "We don't live there anymore, thank God. She kicked us out, remember?"

"She did?" Lulu asked. "Nobody told me."

Squeaky: "Why did she do that?"

Lulu: "We stole all her shit, trashed the place, corrupted her fourteen-year-old daughter, and defecated on the front porch. Sadie did, anyway."

"That wasn't nice," I observed.

"We're feral, man," Charley claimed.

"Look what we found in the wheelie bin," Squeaky said. She pulled out a crate from under the seat. Pears, apples, and oranges. Oh, my!" She bit into a pear. "Rich people won't buy fruit that ain't perfect. So, we grabbed them."

"Dumpster diving."

"Yeah."

"Who knew that fruit grew in wheelie bins? ... Why not just pick them off the trees?"

"We make a little bit of money from the crops we raise.

"Then why eat garbage?"

"We like wheelie bin-diving, that's why!" Squeaky shot back. That settled that.

"We can't help who we are" Charley explained…. "Try two of these."

"What are they?"

"Acid tabs. Very groovy. They'll make the ride seem a little less arduous." He passed tabs around to the other passengers.

"Mmm… Cherry flavored."

"Chewables."

"Want a couple more?"

"I'm good, thanks." In twenty minutes, I was better than good. I was flying. The only problem was that Charlie started looking like the Devil to me.

"You ever seen that silent movie, *Hostel*, man?" Squeaky asked Sandi.

"The one where they torture whores?"

"Yeah, that one. I liked where the pig says, 'Thanks, for having me,' and the bitch says, 'We ain't had you yet, motherfuka,' then cuts a chuck out of the pig's ass and has him for dinner… ha-ha!"

"… Or where they take the cut-off arms and legs and throw them into the furnace."

"I'd like to do that, where we pay pigs to torture them."

"No, man. *We're* the whores; *they're* the pigs, and they pay *us* to torture *them*."

"Why would the pigs pay us to torture them?"

"Because they're pussies. Pigs are pussies. Like the police. They love to be tortured and humiliated... That's why pigs run for president. Or enter beauty contests. Or become professional baseball players... like the Dodgers. They love being humiliated, man."

"We should kill my grandmother," Cappy suggested... "I would like to."

"Why is that?" Squeaky asked.

"It would be fun. Sticking a knife in her. Besides, she owns Barker Ranch. After we kill my grandmother, we can kill off my other relatives and acquire title."

Charlie perked up. "That's a great idea! Barker Ranch is cool, man. And we need a new place to live."

"Then let's do it!" Cappy urged.

"What kind of knives should we use"" Squeaky asked.

"Buck knives."

"No, man," Charlie said. "They're too short, like Pal-Mal Man's dick. A Bowie knife is the way to go."

"Or a vampire knife."

"You're such a squarehead, Squeaky."

Cappy looked deeply into my eyeballs. "You must think I'm a monster," she said lasciviously as she grabbed my crotch.

"Why didn't you kill that senator you arrested?" Charlie asked me. "He could have been easily replaced. A monkey could do his job. Even Squeaky could."

"Senator Mendacious? Why should I? The law will take care of him."

"The law," Charlie said derisively. "Don't tell me about the law. I've spent half of my life in jail, man! I'm suffering here, paying for your sins... So that you can ride your horse... have your birthday parties, fuck bimbos, have what you call a life without being killed...

"I never had a life, man... I don't even know what life is. I go to the fuckin' desert and not even that satisfies you ... I'm no good for anything as far as you're concerned, except to be your sacrificial lamb. Your scapegoat. Every day of my life I've been sacrificed. So, don't tell me about the law, man...You have the right to do this. You have the right to do that... I'll tell you what right you have: you have: the right to be killed. Give up your right to be killed and anything you say can be used against you in a quart of milk."

... That night we all got naked around the campfire. I listened as Charley talked shit about killing pigs and current events.

"Women are good for one thing and one thing only, Assman... "

"Brandon."

"... Receiving dick... Well, maybe cooking, cleaning, washing dishes, scrubbing toilets, and taking the rap when I get in trouble too... Guess what my IQ is... "

"Thirty-five?"

"I didn't say, my age... One hundred and sixty-nine."

"Oh, Charlie, you're so brilliant... You just west wear my poor brain out, Charlie, with your bullshit... Please stop talking because I'm too stupid to follow."

"Listen, "

"Oh, fuck."

"... I'm the only one here who never killed anyone," Charlie said, "except for a few niggas. But that don't count... Now we're supposed to root for the Jews like they're the home team. Whatever happened to that other war that was supposed to be in our vital national interest? ... Ot the prosecution of that Acting President who was trying to overthrow democ-ra-pussy? I guess that ain't so important anymore. I'll tell you what I'm rooting for and that's for the national news media to get pushed into the sea. That's what I'm rooting for. I don't even care which sea."

That motherfuka just would not quit. "Ask him about Helter Skelter," Squeaky suggested.

"That's okay," I replied. (To no avail.)

"Whitey has been feeding blackie his daughters to keep him quiet. We're going to put an end to that, ain't we Squeaky?"

"Tell him how."

"… By relocating all the white bitches of breeding age out to the desert to sleep with me. I'll impregnate them, ensuring the survival of the white race… No need to thank me… Meantime, blackie can get off his ass and start killing off whitey due to his sexual frustration. Then when blackie takes over and be trippin' because he don't know what to do, I'll be there to take over. I'll rule the world! … Are you with me or against me, Assman? There's no in-between."

This motherfuka was insane. I had the feeling the women (of which I'd loosely consider Squeaky to be one) had listened to this bullshit plenty of times before.

"Hard to say. I've been feeling indecisive as of late." That there was no lie.

I don't know how, but Charlie knew about how I killed Pimperton. As sure as we smoked our reefers, he kept reminding me about it and making me feel bad about myself.

Squeaky knew what I was going through because she said, "Brandon, may the Devil give you strength to face another day... Let me help you with that dick." She unbuttoned my trousers.

"How did you two meet?"

"Me and Charlie? ...Well, uh..." She laughed. "Let's say, on the beach."

"What do you think of Gypsy over there?"

"You want to fuck her?"

"I wouldn't mind."

"Well, she's a liar and a con artist. But she's articulate; she speaks well..."

"Uh-huh..."

"She's a girl..."

"I can see that."

"... She helps with everything... cleans up... cooks... sucks cock... like girls do."

There was a sameness about all these girls. Same flat tones of voice and lack of distinct personalities.

"What else does she like to do?"

"Fuck... She's a sensitive lover."

"I can see that... the way she's playing with her pussy..."

"She sends us kisses on the raindrops."

"Aww... What a lovely thing to say."

"Thank you!"

"See, you ain't all evil."

"Bad enough."

The flames of the campfire lit up her smiling face and beautiful, red hair."

"You're adorable!"

"I know, right?"

"Let's fuck."

"Okay..."

SURFER, SOLDIER, POLYGAMIST, JERK

The day was magic. The night was even better… Virginia was loving her Santa Cruz honeymoon although she wasn't quite sure why she had married Lloyd Sweety.

Being anxious to get out of Bodie after surreptitiously lynching Virginia's two-year-old son, Everitt who had started the fire that burned down the town, Lloyd had insisted upon a quickie-ceremony.

Somewhere over the Sierra Nevada Mountains, the newlyweds had gotten robbed on the train that was headed west to Santa Cruz. The bandits, former Sheriff, Johnny Behen and Lizzie Bordone, wore masks and couldn't be identified.

But that was all behind them. Virginia and Lloyd were now on the beach soaking up the rays while watching the sexy Hawaiian princes demonstrate the sport of surfing.

As Virginia applied sunscreen to her 98% naked body, Lyman Swale, sitting on a blanket a few feet away with his wife. Antoinette kept looking over at her.

Antoinette was the baby daughter of Hawaiian bigamist, Francisco de Paula Marín, a remarkable Spaniard who had deserted the ship early in the nineteenth century and migrated to Hawaii where he acquired property around Honolulu and became an advisor to Hawaiian King, Kamehameha I. Marin also achieved fame as a horticulturist and sired twenty-seven or so offspring by four wives, with Antoinette being his last child.

She had married Lyman who turned out to be a crook. Wanted for counterfeiting in Hawaii, Lyman and his family fled the island for Santa Cruz, California where they established roots. Being childless, the King and Queen of Hawaii had adopted the King's nephews -- the three surfer dudes -- who were head of the line for succession to the throne.

Jonah, known as Cupid, the baby of the three, was the charming and athletic one. He loved baseball, football, surfing, cycling, rowing, and even hula dancing, A fierce nationalist, he would later be sentenced to prison for fighting with rebel forces opposed to the U.S. takeover of Hawaii.

Koa, the eldest, was the ultimate beach bum. After completing his education in the U.S. and England, he joined the diplomatic service in Hawaii and co-founded the Hawaiian Democratic Party.

Edward was smaller than his brothers and sickly. He could be difficult to get along with. After his days in Santa Cruz, he wouldn't last long. He contracted typhoid fever and died in Hawaii at age 18.

But on this magnificent day, all of that was in the unforeseeable future. The city band played while tourists and townsfolk alike frolicked in the surf. There was an ocean swimming contest. A local theater group performed on the wet sand.

But every eye, it seemed, was trained on the princes, riding their long, redwood o'lo boards in the surf, a sight not previously seen on the mainland.

Eavesdropping on the conversation next to her, Virginia surmised that the princes were staying with the elite Swale family during their time in Santa Cruz.

"Aren't they wonderful? Virginia said to Antoinette.

She looked over. "Mmm…. Yes and no,"

"Is it true they're all brothers?"

"Cupid, Kao, and Edward are. Martin is their cousin. He already has thirteen children by three wives.

"Oh, my!"

Lloyd was trimming his nails and only half paying attention when Lyman crawled over to him.

"The breakers at the mouth of the river are very fine, no?"

Lloyd looked up. "No… I mean, yes. Very fine."

"Interested in a little action tonight?" Lyman asked.

"Oh, no. Me and Virginia are here on our honeymoon."

"Excellent! We'll make it one you won't soon forget. How much money you got?"

"Only about a thousand dollars. We got robbed on the train."

"Can I have it?"

"What?"

"I need a thousand dollars to buy party favors."

"… Those boys look good stripped," Antoinette spoke confidentially to Virginia, "and they fuck good too, but that Edward is a nasty little cuss."

"What do you mean?"

"He and my husband, Lyman got into it this morning. Edward asked Lyman for money. Of course, my husband said he didn't have any. Edward flew into a rage and called Lyman a cheap, counterfeiting con artist."

"How rude!"

"That's what I thought. I hate him. I love Cupid and Kao however. They are so sweet."

"What about Martin?" Virginia asked, squinting out to sea.

"My nephew? Oh, that man is a snake charmer. He can make anything grow. Especially babies. He's quite virulent…"

"I'd better not fuck him then."

"… And a nice guy too…. Martin has developed new kinds of fruits and vegetables on the islands, established the first grape vineyard, distilled sugarcane into rum, cultivated the first pineapple and cotton, mango, and orange crops…"

"You're making me hungry."

"Then you should come bred with us. I'm Antonette, by the way."

"Virginia. And this man trimming his nails is my new husband, Lloyd. We're here on our honeymoon."

"Well, you should drop by for dinner tonight, 231 Cathcart Street, and meet the princes. My family is all inbred."

Virginia felt a tingle in her lower region.

"Well, it beats fucking Lloyd all night long."

A bonfire cracked on the beach. As night fell, Lloyd, Virginia, and their new friends retired to Lyman and Antoinette's place.

Further down the beach, a fat, out-of-work American politician by the name of Goober Cleveland, who had a face like a walrus, was romancing -- even seducing -- the Queen of Hawaii, Lili'uokalani. or just Lydia.

"Look at that spectacle out there, Lydia. The heirs to the throne are finally calling it a day."

"They're just boys. My poor, dead brother, Kalākaua's barren wife's nephews. Kalākaua taught them to surf.

"Pity the Hawaiian royal families can't seem to produce an heir and must turn to super doper surfer babies instead,"

"There's a lot of intrigue and in-fucking that goes on in Hawaii, for sure," responded the Queen. "It's a magical place."

"Sounds like it… Love is in the air here too. Look at all the couples fornicating on the sand. We should be doing that… You must produce an heir, Lydia. Otherwise, American companies will take over your country. Hawaii is strategic to American national interests, notwithstanding being a garden of Eden agriculturally.

"True."

"I know your husband is not well… You're so beautiful." Their lips met. "You must get preggy before he joins his ancestors."

"He's white. He doesn't have anchovies… I mean, ancestors."

The three princes plus their cousin brought marijuana spiked with LSD to the party, which was unsurprising considering that Santa Cruz was becoming the weed capital of California. Virginia, Lloyd, the surfer princes, Martin, Lyman, and Antoinette sat around the sunken living room getting loaded, talking, and laughing.

After a while, Cupid offered to show Virginia around the house. He took her into a bedroom that was trimmed in gold. They got naked on the bed… Cupid slipped inside of her. Then his brothers were inside of her as well.

"I plant my seed in you so it will spout," Martin said.

"He's known for having a green dick," Cupid explained.

"I plant mine for good luck with your marriage," Koa added.

"You'd better not have given me the clap," Edward threatened as he pulled out.

Virginia wasn't listening. Her mind was conjuring visions of island life. She felt so relaxed as the princes continued pleasuring her.

… In the living room, Lloyd was tastefully eating out Antonette while Lyman was fucking him up the ass. It wasn't to be the last time Lloyd would be fucked over that evening.

… On the beach, Goober rocked his cock in Queen Lydia's pussy, his fat gut hanging loosely over her hers… Then she turned over and assumed the position on her hands and knees, allowing the walrus to fuck her doggie.

Tourists joined in, taking turns balling the Hawaiian Queen while Goober got underneath to suck her hanging fruit.

"Oh, that's good,", the Queen said. "Don't stop… Put that white sperm in me."

"They are fucking you, Queen Lili'uokalani, to symbolize the relationship between America and Hawaii."

"It's okay. One day planes will fly over Hawaii and bomb your battleships for what you are doing now."

"Arranged marriage has always been the custom among our people," Chief Liggy-gaga said to his top-naked daughter.

"But, Daddy, I don't want to marry that old motherfuka."

"You must, Yaawa, to prevent war between our pimples... I mean, people. The Imedin are rising – they've already been seen eating a white man -- and we Yackels must sacrifice your happiness and your titties which are getting so big, by the way with my sucking on them. I appreciate that in a young maiden."

"I am no longer a maiden, Daddy. Vevuk and I have done it lots of times."

"That's okay too. Bitch, don't you know you can have your cake with Vevuk and eat out your old husband's ass every night too?"

"But I don't want to eat out any old man's ass. Please, Daddy. I want to marry Vevuk. He loves me and I love him more."

"It is forbidden."

"But, Daddy, you know that old man is nasty."

"Look, daughter, I've got more to worry about than your bullshit problem. John Frum is coming here today with Cargo for our village."

"John Frum?"

"John Frum America."

"Oh, *that* John Frum."

"So, I need you to be a good girl. Run along, have fun, but don't get preggy."

Deep in thought, Yaawa walked up the forest hill to the edge of the cliff where she could look down upon the vast ocean… She saw a ship coming into port.

… Waawa watched as Lloyd was manhandled off the ship and brought in front of her father.

"Welcome to Tanna, John Frum," Liggy-gaga said. It's about damn time you got here. We've waited years for your return since your departure during the Spanish/American war. I still remember you promising the Yackel people goodies in return for America turning Tanna females into Comfort Women for your soldiers. So where are the goodies?"

"I don't know what the fuck you're talking about… I was doped, fucked silly, and shanghaied in Santa Cruz, then dispatched to this godforsaken place because some surfer dudes wanted to ball my lovely new wife... well, new to me, anyway."

.... Yaawa ran down the hill away from the village, over to the next village where Vevuk, her beloved, lived. Yaawa found him in his little grass hut balling her older sister, Petuni.

"Petuni! What the fuck! I told you I loved Vevuk. So, why are you balling my beloved?"

"I figured if he was that good, I should get some for myself."

"You've always been the naughty one, Petuni. Come, Vevuk. We must get off the island before war breaks out."

War... What is it good for? Absol-pollutely nothin'! Leave me alone." He went back to balling Petuni.

Yaawa ran out of the hut in tears. She saw Tanna warriors running through the forest carrying a long Yucca branch from which Lloyd Sweety hung upside down. He looked like a pig, bound to it by his wrists and ankles. Yaawa kept running until she reached her village and met her friend, Suri.

"Where are you going in such a hurry, Yaawa?"

"To America to find an overbearing jerk like Father, join a cult, and take my life to the next level."

"Good luck with that."

"Thank you."

Yaawa swiped a canoe and paddled out to the ship which was raising anchor in the harbor. She was helped aboard just before onrushing Imedin warriors began attacking it.

… As for Lloyd Sweety, he was boiled alive in a big pot like a red lobster for failing to keep the promise that John Frum America had made in vain many years ago.

White Man in the Black Hat

Gypsy came over to join us. "What do you think of JC?"

"JC?"

"Charlie. He says he lived 2000 years ago as JC and died on the cross. He's the reincarnation of Jesus Christ."

"He's not… Oh, he died on the cross alright, according to Madame Koolista, but not as Jesus Christ. His name back then was Jake Crapper. He wore glasses and tried to act smart."

"You mean that Charlie wasn't Jesus Christ?" Gypsy asked.

"No, man. Sorry."

"Well, then who was Jesus Christ?"

"Katie Davy."

"Ain't that a bitch?"

"Oh, she ain't so bad… Well, Lech Christian thought he was. But he was only Mary Magdalene."

"Why did Jesus Christ come back as Katie Davy?"

"To get some dick, according to Madame Koolista."

"That's crazy!"

"Yeah." … So, instead of listening to that hater, Charlie, blather on to the others, I fucked Squeaky and Gypsy by the campfire.

Both girls had great bodies in different ways. Squeaky was the perfect cult nympho while older Gypsy had a full woman's body that was to die for. I was lucky I didn't. Charlie held a knife to my stomach while I was inside of Gypsy and kept asking me if he should stick it in. He went through a series of scary faces.

"Not right now. I'm busy,"

"Kill him when I start to orgasm," Gypsy said.

Fortunately, just before she did," Charlie passed out.

…I awoke to the sweet smell of breakfast cooking over the fire… Squeaky brought me a plate.

"Hungry?"

"For you."

"From what we pulled out of the wheelie bin, I made you a nice bacon, lettuce, and tomato sandwich."

"For me? I asked sleepily.

"Try it."

"… Mmm, good."

"You like it?"

"I love it." "She smiled. "This is delicious, Squeaky. You are so amazing."

"Want another?"

"Sure." She brought it and I gulped that one down too."

The others were moving to the stage. "… Well, time to go."

"Sure." I wiped my mouth and rose to my feet.

"… What if you just consumed ten tabs of acid?"

… Regaining consciousness, I found myself buried up to my neck in a graveyard. Fire Ants and beetles were crawling over my honey-covered face. The stage and Mansion Family were gone.

Things had been going so well. How had I lost the initiative?

I was now faced with an existential problem for which I could think of only one possible solution...

"Help!" I cried out weakly. "Help!"

I drifted into a hallucination...

The big, white man in the black hat jumped out of the carriage that had pulled up outside the Benedict Canyon mansion. He shimmied up the phone pole and cut the line... His three bitches stepped out of the carriage. The man climbed down the pole, approached the carriage, and had words for the three women. The chunky one stayed by the carriage as a lookout. The other two, along with the man, approached the house and stepped onto the front porch. The man creepy crawled the house through the window and unlocked the door from inside. His bitches flowed into the house. The man whispered to the prettier of the two women who went up the stairs with her accomplice... The intruder went to the couch where a man was sleeping. A kick to the head woke him up.

"Who are you?" the man asked.

"The Devil come to do the Devil's work."

...If you're feeling unresolved joy, either resolve it or Prevelin will resolve it for you. Prevelin is made by Todd, a paramedic firefighter. "I was looking for a way to make money,

so I invented Prevelin. My annual income has increased by 143.25%. So, keep buying it, sucker." ... What a bummer! When did they start putting commercials in acid trips? I wondered...

... The two women brought three housemates – a beautiful, pregnant woman, her friend, and her former lover – down the stairs at knifepoint and into the front room... The white man in the black hat tied the pregnant woman and her former lover together by their necks. He threw the other end of the rope over an open beam and secured it. The bound man complained about the rough treatment being accorded the pregnant woman.

"What? You don't have enough money, you fuckin' pig?" The still-conscious objector was shot by the tall assailant and then stabbed seven times... The unbound woman was led upstairs to fetch her purse... The man who had been kicked in the head had his hands tied together by the pretty intruder... He broke loose and struggled with the pretty woman who stabbed him several times in the leg... He got to his feet and ran out onto the front porch. The big man followed and hit him in the head several times with the butt of the gun, stabbed him repeatedly, and shot him twice.

The stocky girl by the carriage ran toward the front porch.

Upstairs, the woman with the purse escaped out the bedroom door and ran toward the pool... The plain girl chased her to the lawn and stabbed her. The big man ran down the porch and helped stab the woman to death.

The mortally wounded man on the porch struggled across the lawn. The man in the black hat tracked him down and finished him off with the knife.

Inside, the pregnant woman pleaded for her life and the life of her unborn child.

"Take me hostage. Just let me live until I can have my baby. Then you can do whatever you want to me."

The bad man and the pretty girl stabbed her sixteen times, then hung her by the neck until dead.

I was brought back to my senses by a little girl who was wiping the ants off my face. She put a canteen to my lips and gave me a sip of water.

"Thank you," I whispered. "Do you have an older sister?"

"That can be arranged."

I lapsed back into another horrible hallucination.

It was the next evening... The white man in the black hat was carrying a bayonet up the front steps. He passed Charlie in the doorway. Charlie turned. "Do it right this time," he said, before continuing down the steps... The man resting on the sofa was roused, at gunpoint, by the intruder, who handed him a leather rope with which to bind his hands.

...If you're feeling unresolved joy, either resolve it or Prevelin will resolve it for you. Prevelin is made by Todd, a paramedic firefighter. "I was looking for a way to make money so I invented Prevelin,.. My annual income has increased by 143.25%. So, keep buying it, suckers." That fucker again... I wish he'd get out of my head.

... The plain woman from the night before entered the house along with a tall, new female accomplice. The two women went into the bedroom and came back with the wife... Pillowcases were pulled over the couple's head and then secured with cords from new-fangled electric lamps. The women were instructed by the man to take the wife back into the bedroom, which they did... The hooded husband was stabbed in the throat by the man with the bayonet. The commotion could be heard from the bedroom... The bad man investigated. He saw the hooded wife swinging the lamp attached to her neck at her assailants. The bad man stabbed the wife with his bayonet and then returned to the front room, stabbing the husband twelve more times. He paused to carve the phrase "FUCK THE WAR IN ISREAL. THAT'S THEIR PROBLEM, NOT OURS" into the man's abdomen. It took him a few minutes.

The assailant returned to the bedroom and found his plain cohort stabbing the wife with a kitchen knife. Blood spurted out, which got the hairy woman excited. The tall, new girl repeatedly stabbed the now lifeless body in the back and abdomen.

"She's done," the now completely ugly murderess said.

"Stick a fork in her," said the new girl. So, the one with the hair on her chest did.

"And a steak knife too."

The hairy murderous did that too and, at the same time, climaxed.

Bed-Hopping in D-Ward

I made the second biggest mistake of my life (the first involved deciding to be born). I agreed to fly back to Reno with the fucking Wright Brothers.

I wanted to file charges against Lecher Christian for hitting me over the head and stealing my woman in a shithole Reno Whorehouse.

I also wanted Brandon Assman arrested for the murder of Cecil Fergoosen, even if he didn't do it. Third, but not least, I needed to find Lizzie Bordone and get some pussy from her.

"But Johnny," the novice pilot, Orville Rickenbacker Wright said, "Reno is so far away. Let me and my brother fly you there in our new single-propeller Liberty Eagle. It's perfectly safe."

"Sure. Why not? It's only my life... Your flight record is spotty at best, Wright, and lethal at worst."

"But we've always managed to bail out ahead of any crash and the Liberty Eagle is new and improved. Besides, we'll be flying the southern route this time where they didn't build the mountains as high up off the ground."

"Are you stoned?"

"No."

"Licensed?"

"Our brothel is, sure."

"I mean, do you have an aeronautics license?"

"A what? We flunked out of flight school but continue having nightmares about it, so we're thinking about flying all the time... Not to mention—"

"Then don't mention it."

Although he did seem remorseful about their recent failures and I wanted to stick it to Lech Christian for ruining my hustle, Orville's argument was less than convincing... But my life had already been ruined by being born, so I agreed to give it a chance.

Sure enough, we crashed around Waco after the brothers had bailed. I wound up in the lunatic asylum there with two broken arms, two broken legs, a broken pelvis, cracked ribs, third-degree burns, and only my dick and tongue sticking out of the body cast. That last part was my idea which I got from President Hardening. Now there was a President. Not at all like that creep, Ball that we've got in there now who can't speak for lying.

I recognized two of the nurses, Carolyn and Nancy who had been involved in McArthur's Comfort Women Program in Ventura and whom I had already enjoyed the privilege of fucking. It was a lot harder now... my dick, that is. And the two ladies made a nice meal of it. I loved how they played with their food while I Face-Sat them. They signed my body cast too.

I, Ned McLain, do solemnly swear—Well, no. On second thought, I'm not going to do that anymore. The last time I tried it in front of the Senate oversight committee, I lied my ass off and was sentenced five-to-ten at Leavenworth.

But a whole shitload of new mental patients showed up uninvited one night, having been deported from the 21st century.

The neighborhood dogs knew something was up, if the people inside didn't. The dogs howled at every deep breath the newcomers made as they forced their way into D Ward, found beds and bedmates, and mostly fell sound asleep, exhausted from their involuntary passage.

Only I couldn't sleep So, I got out of bed, walked down the hall, and peeked into the nursing station. The two new hires, Carolyn Harrington and Nancy Priminger were balling Dr. Truelover. *The staff will be tied up for a while*, I thought. I decided to bed-check the facility for myself, first checking the common area and kitchen. I found patients there that I already knew. Like Admiral Nimnutz, Epiphany Fargo, and Girlie Brown. Ted Potter and Jack Holmes were enjoying a midnight snack together. It appeared they all would be up a while longer.

I proceeded down the hall and began peeking into the darkened rooms. Zelda was asleep but who was that in bed with her? A strange-looking police uniform was draped over the chair. I would have to ask Zelda about that in the morning.

I looked in on Ashley O'Foole. She was under the covers with this creepy-looking guy. I held up an electric hand torch to illuminate the room. Ashley sat up and blinked her eyes. The man was snoring in bed next to her. "Oh, hi, Ned. This is Lawrence Lizard-Lounge. He just arrived from the future and needed a place to sack out so I said he could sleep with me."

I frowned. "Oh, okay, Ashley. Just checking to see if you're all right. I heard the dogs barking outside. Lizard-Lounge looks like one of them."

I checked in on crazy Bethany T. The T stood for Trouble. She had recently been held at the Joss House in Rock Springs pending her murder trial. Now she was in bed with an old man who looked like Ichabod Crane.

"Who you got there, Bethany?"

"He said his name was Brother Robbie and that he's a preacher. That's all I know. Watch this space."

"Which space? The one between your legs?"

"Yes, please."

The pattern continued. Maddie was in bed with a Dr. Jacoff while Penelope Hurst was pressing the flesh with Miss. Goodbody.

"The poor child was traumatized by her journey," Penelope explained. "So, I ate her pussy." *Liberal sociopath*, I thought.

"Very kind of you, Mrs. Hurst," was all I said.

Maddie was fucking Dr. Jacoff. "Oh, I'm such a whore," she explained. Emily Showers was sitting at a table. She claimed to be plotting her revenge on the man who killed her brother in Bodie, Brandon Assman, who I'd never heard of. But I don't get around much anymore.

The new residents, for the most part, seem to be assimilating well, I thought as I returned to the nurse's station to provide another dick for the staff orgy. I knew from experience just how insatiable Carolyn Herringer and Nancy Preminger could be and questioned whether the bisexual Dr. Truelover could adequately handle these two nymphos by himself. I felt that professional ethics required me to intervene. I just couldn't remember which profession I had ever been involved with.

I'm a quick healer. With Carolyn and Nancy's help, I was up and taking baby steps in no time. I met this crazy motherfuka, Adam, on one of my jaunts. Nice guy, handsome, but insecure. I told him what happened to me with the Wright Brothers and how I wanted to sue them.

Adam said his Daddy ran a gay cult in Virginia City called the Ponderosa. It seems Daddy was rich and knew all the best people. Adam expressed bitterness over how he'd been disinherited, kicked off the Ponderosa, and institutionalized here at Waco simply for being straight and sneaking chicks onto the Ponderosa.

He told me about his cute girlfriend, Mary Ann Wells, who still lived there alongside the gay guys. Adam suggested I tune in, turn on, drop in, and rip them off. I didn't have time, but I promised to check it out if I was ever in the neighborhood. I did want to meet this Mary Ann and my stock portfolio in San Francisco wasn't doing so great.

Get Thee to a Nunnery, Amelia

Father Luis Cervantes had a problem. He couldn't get Sister Amelia off his mind. He'd been smitten ever since first laying eyes on her at St Deuteronomy's parish in Waco. Father Cervantes had good taste. Sister Amelia was smokin' hot like Jalapeno Peppers straight out of the oven. She had been living lease-free in his head. He knew that if he didn't get paid some rent from her soon, he'd have to take it out in trade before someone else did.

Leaning back in the confessional, Father Cervantes was half listening to this old bitch confess how she failed to help some guy in a typewriting class when he blurted out, "That's enough! I'm sick of it! Go and fuck somebody your size. Then come back here and tell me about it while I jerk off."

"Father!" the woman gasped. "ain't you had your little boy today?"

"You bore me." That was true enough. "Git the fuck out of here!" He stepped out of the box and stalked down the hall to his office where he called his porn star friend, Poison Penis-Envie, and asked her to come to confess something while he pleasured himself.

"Father," she explained. "I'm not that girl anymore...I'm proud of what I do."

"And what may I ask is that?

"Provide sex addiction therapy."

"Fine. Be that slut."

"You act like it's a sin for a woman to have a pussy."

"I'll meet you for coffee at Joe Blowjob's Bar and Grill in twenty minutes."

"… Luis. How the fuck are you?"

"Okay, I guess."

"Something is bothering you. I can tell."

"Oh, so you're a psychic now in addition to being a sex therapist."

"As a matter of fact, yes."

"Anything to drink?" the short, bi0-boobed waitress asked.

"Just holy water….I mean, water."

"Sure." She left.

"I don't get to order… Fine… I'm retired from porno, Luis,".

"When the fuck did this great transformation occur?"

"On Tuesday."

"It's Wednesday now. So, you've been clean for, like twelve hours?"

"Fourteen."

"Oh, fourteen. Well, more power to you," he said grimly.

"Father, I hope you're not going to force me to question my faith. I'm perfectly capable of turning Buddhist on your ass."

"You always were Buddhist anyway, whore."

"Trick."

"Ass-wiper."

The girl came back with the water. Her tits fell out of her bodice as she bent over to set the water down. "Oh, my!"

"Uh, bimbo…" The horny priest stuffed a nipple into his mouth. "Thanks for the olive," he said, chewing on it thoughtfully.

"Mind taking my order?" Poison asked with disdain in her voice.

"What's your name?" Luis asked the waitress.

"Layla."

"That seems appropriate. Layla. You've got the face of an angel."

"And the body of a fat pig," Poison added. "Your body is not at all good as mine,"

"Few bodies are," Father Cervantes affirmed.

"Is there something on your alleged mind, Father? Or did you just come to this dump for the atmosphere, insults, and nipples?"

"It's Sister Amelia. She seems too good to be true. Can't take my mind off of her. She'd be like heaven to touch. I want to hold her so much. At long last love has arrived. Don't know from whence it derived. She's just too good to be true. Can't take my mind off of her."

"I see," Poison said soberly.

"Oh, the way that I stare, there's nothing else to compare. The sight of her leaves me weak. There are no words left to speak."

"Well, if you feel like you feel, at least let her know that it's real,"

"She's just too good to be true. Can't take my mind off of her."

Poison's panties were getting moist. "Sounds like you've got it bad."

"It sure does," Layla said, slipping her hand down her skirt."

Sister Amelia was saying her rosary as she shook the beads… "Heavenly Father, full of grace, hollow be thy name. If only I had a dick, I could make so much money fucking cops up the ass." Then it came to her like an angel from heaven. *A strap-on would pay for itself in no time.* So, she went to see Mother Superior and explained how she needed to be excused to buy some poverty pills because she had been feeling kind of hungry lately.

"And git you some birth control ones too, sista girl. I want no babies on my watch. Know what I mean?" the big black Mother Superior responded.

"Yes, big booty momma." *Jesus,* Sister Amelia thought. *Now I got to hit up big pharma as well as the sex shop, all in one morning.*

... Walking into the church with his head down, Father Cervantes ran over Sister Amelia on her way out the door. They both went sprawling with Father Cervantes on top and his dick swelling rapidly. "I think I bruised myself down there." Father Cervantes observed.

"I'm fine, thanks," the sister replied sarcastically.

"My balls is on fire."

"At least you got balls and a dick to catch on fire and get bruised."

"I'm sorry you are so ill-equipped, Sister. But as Freud once noted--"

"I don't give a fuck what Freud once noted. Now get off me! This is creepy. Reminds me of how my father, a police officer, used to do it."

"But I ain't that guy. I love you, Sister, Can't take my mind off of you. Don't that mean nothin' to you?" he asked, feeling her titties by force of habit.

"It means you're dick dirty cuz you say that to all the nuns."

"What's your fantasy?"

"Getting you the fuck off me. Now let me go!" Amelia struggled to her feet.

"I'll pray for you," Luis promised as she ran out the door.

Mother Superior heard the shouting from down the hall and hurried to the scene of the crime…"What the fuck you doing on the floor, Father?"

"Praying for Sister Amelia… Jesus says…"

"I know what Jesus says, and he don't say nothin' about raping nuns on the floor of the cathedral."

"He say, 'let the little children come all over me.'"

"Not in them exact words, he didn't…Why don't you get wit' a real woman?" she asked, squatting down on his bruised dick.

"Nooo!" But it was too late.

"Keep yer voice down, cracker. Don't make me slap you." So, Father Cervantes decided to submit to the will of God, or at least content himself with Mother Superior's unique brand of nursing.

… No sooner had Sister Amelia entered the pharmacy than she heard, "Debbie!" and looked up.

"Poison." *Great*, Amelia thought. *This big-mouth, tell-all-of-my-business bitch. Now I'll never make it to the sex store.*

"I ain't seen you in forever."

"It's Amelia now."

"Everybody misses you. How's the nun gig going?"

"It's alright. I've been clean for 6 months."

"Two days for me."

"What are you doing here?"

"Buying condoms for my dog." Sister Amelia stared at her. "We should do a threesome."

"I can't. I'm off dick."

"My God! Congratulations! How did you manage that?"

"I just love Jesus with all my heart, all my mind, all my soul, and rely on my dildo."

"There's something I've got to talk to you about."

"Concerning Father Cervantes?"

"How did you know? ... Tomorrow at four. The Jungle Room. Be there."

... The Jungle Room was made up to be the Amazon Forest. Lit candleholders on the walls. Exotic birds screech in the potted trees. Wildlife dying. A dead elk lay in the middle of the lounge. "Wonder how long that's been there?" Poison mused.

"All of God's creatures are sacred."

"That sacred one starting to smell. Maybe we shouldn't order the steak."

"Careful your hair doesn't catch on fire."

"Holy shit! No pun intended."

"What have you been doing, Poison?"

"Working. Well, directing. I retired from performing. I've got this idea for a nun scene…"

"Oh, no… I'm so done with that."

"Did I offer you a role?"

"Jesus wouldn't like it."

"Who's this Jesus you keep referring to? Yer pimp or something?"

"My lord and master."

"Sounds kinky."

"Would you ladies be interested in a cock's tail?" "

"Didn't I see you at Joe's the other day?"

"I work here now."

"I'll have a sidecar. Make it a double. You owe me for last time."

Layla turned to Sister Amelia. "Oh, nothing for me, thanks."

"She'll have a sidecar too. Light on the lemon juice; heavy on the cognac."

"It's your funeral."

"You ever sell pussy?"

"What girl hasn't?" She looked at Amelia. "Present company accepted, of course… You have big boobs like me, Sister. She pulled out one of Amelia's to examine it. "Bite marks,"

"Just bring our fuckin' drinks," Poison said crossly.

"I got to make 'em first," Layla responded indignantly before stalking off.

"She gets around," Poison asserted. "Probably escorts. She could play a big-boob waitress who gets fucked… I had lunch with Father Cervantes the other day. Or maybe it was breakfast…All he could talk about was you."

"That's nice. Hope he didn't say anything bad."

"Bad is how he wants you."

"Yeah?"

" Seems to me that a man of the cloth should keep his dick in his pants unless he's got something to show off.".

"Yer such a hypocrite, Poison."

"I ain't so bad. Just earthy, you know? ... Remember that time we worked together."

"No! I mean... I'm trying to forget about all that."

"You sure you won't do one more shoot?"

"Oh, I just couldn't... What's it pay?"

Poison looked around surreptitiously like she didn't want anybody to know how much silent porno stars make. Then she wrote a number on a piece of paper and slid it across the table. "I put the address and call time for you too." Sister Amelia read the paper and slipped it into her purse.

Layla brought the drinks and turned to go.

"Wait." Poison scribbled another note, wrapped it in a dollar bill, and jammed it it between Layla's' titties and down her bodice. "And bring two different color nun outfits, very revealing ones."

"I don't know," Layla mused.

"Being in silent porno is the best way to let men know you're available, whore."

That's about when Lawrence Lizard-Lounge came over and started singing in the ladies' faces...

"*I love you, baby.*

And want to fuck you so bad.

I mean, so good.

I need you, baby.

All the lonely night

I wanna fuck you, baby.

Trust in me when I say…"

"What should I bring?" Sister Amelia asked.

"Father Cervantes and a strap-on… Get away, motherfuka!" Poison scolded Lizard-Lounge. "Don't make me slap you."

Death Valley Girls

Every day, this groundhog would dig his way up to the surface just a few feet from my head, look out over the tombstones, and say, "You think you're clever, Devil. But I'm on to you. Nothin' has changed. It's all one big pile of shit." …. The Devil would answer back, "I need every one of you." The groundhog would retort: "You think I ain't smart enough to recognize a lie like that?" … Then he'd come out of the hole, then peer into it. "As for you groundhogs, you ain't changed either. You can still go fuck yourselves!" I would look at him and beg, "Mr. Groundhog. As you can see, I'm buried up to my neck. You dig?" "Not unless I have to." …. "You're a groundhog. I know you can do it. I'll pay whatever you say." The groundhog would get this thoughtful look, survey the holes all over the graveyard, and say, "I got too much competition and no spare time." Then he'd dart back down into his hole.

After the bitches, Sadie, Katie, Linda, Lulu, and I killed the beautiful, preggy actress and all the other rich piggies on two successive nights of wanton violence and debauchery, I decided to take a break from the Family and head back to Texas to get a haircut and visit my parents.

I had no money, no job, no transportation, and no hope for the future. So, I called my mother. She offered to wire $200 if I consented to a buzz cut. Reluctantly, I agreed.

Unfortunately, on the first night of my journey, I misplaced the money at a Death Valley whorehouse… in Darwin, I believe it was…. Or spent it. I don't remember which exactly. Too many drugs.

I took a job with Borax as a twenty-mule-team driver… That took me out to Amargosa where I met Norma and her no-good pimp/paramour, Frank Savage. Both Norma and Frank were married to other people. Norma grew up in Nebraska, moved to Seattle as a youngster, got married against her parents' wishes, moved back to Nebraska with her new husband, and then soon relocated to the bawdy town of Arrow, Colorado. Norma's husband, Clinton, got arrested on a forgery rap and asked his friend, Frank Skinner, a local gambler, to keep his wife company. What could go wrong?

Frank kept Norma company alright. He also kept her busy turning tricks at Dirty Dick's Saloon and Whorehouse.

Frank was a restless sort. Soon the new couple was on the move again, visiting one mining camp after another before finally settling in Rhyolite, Nevada which is located adjacent to Death Valley.

Frank and Norma were a pair to draw to; both had bad tempers. Crazy for each other and passionate in every way, they would get drunk and tear up the town. Sometimes, Frank would beat Norma. Only they would make up with a wild night of carousing and lovemaking. Norma made enough money to acquire half-interest in a saloon next to the Mission Hotel. Fred attached a crib to the saloon. Norma would sleep in one half with her johns while the swarthy, broad-shouldered Savage slept in the attached room (often with prostitutes) with only a thin wall separating Frank from Norma and her evening companion.

One morning, she woke up with a miner who had paid her $20 for the night but asked for $5 back so he could buy breakfast and a train ticket out of town.

Norma agreed from the goodness of her black heart. The man walked over to the hotel where he had breakfast and then blew his brains out.

Somehow, Frank was accused of the man's death. A judge ordered him jailed until a grand jury could be convened in two weeks. The grand jury ultimately cleared Fred of wrongdoing due to a lack of evidence.

But Frank was furious with the judge for having been jailed for two weeks. So, he asked the judge to join him for a drink. Once the two were in the bar, Frank slugged the old judge in the mouth.

Savage was placed under arrest and promptly sentenced to six months in the Tonopah jail. Norma went back to work but, feeling increasing harassment from the authorities, decided to move on to Amargosa, California in the Mohave Desert,

She wrote to Frank, ...*I am going to work down there and will find work for you. If I can get any other work in Amargosa, it's no more tenderloin for me. It just doesn't pay.*

Amargosa is where I met Norma and got to know her quite well, becoming her protector in the absence of Frank, with whom she continued a loving correspondence.

Norma went to work at the Adobe Dance Hall where she drank and smoked and carried on like a wildcat. had cold eyes but a hot temper, especially when she was drinking. At age 22, her profane vocabulary was second to none.

I was back and forth with the mule team from one end of Death Valley to the other. I still intended to return to Texas to get a buzz cut, but I had to build up a stake first. I didn't think much about them two insane nights in Los Angeles; I was having too much fun chasing Norma and other whores. There was a policeman in Amargosa, but he didn't amount to much.

Norma rented a cottage on Main Street where I stayed with her many a night in the prickly heat and my prick spent a good amount of time in her oven too.

But all good things must come to an end. One day, Frank returned, whether with permission or on his initiative, I ain't sure.

She introduced us. "This is the man in the black hat I wrote you about, Frank."

The three of us raised hell that night, celebrating Frank's freedom. It was fun while it lasted.

We went to one saloon for a meal... another for drinks... and a third for Irish Creme De Menthe Cocktails. Then we made our way to the Mission bar.

Norma, who said she wasn't feeling well, lagged.

At the Mission, Frank insisted that Norma drink beer. Norma said she didn't want to drink beer and Frank got mad. So, she drank the beer. But when Frank insisted that she swallow the foam, she put her foot down... From the other side of the bar, Frank threw a glass that struck her in the shoulder. He threw another glass which she deflected with her hand. He rushed up to her... "No, Frank," she said. But he struck her. She fell to her knees. Then he kicked her. She got up and ran to the door. He called her all kinds of filthy names. She asked for permission to return home. He assented and she kissed him goodnight.

I got Frank more-or-less settled down over a few more beers.

"You shouldn't beat her up like that, Frank," I said. "She's a good girl... a little high-spirited is all."

Lovely too, in my opinion.

"Good for shit," was his reply. "She's used to it."

I accompanied Frank back to the cottage and bade him goodnight. He started to get sentimental.

"I love you, man."

"I love you too, Frank."

"I can't thank you enough for looking after Norma while I was away."

"It was my pleasure." I wasn't lying about that.

Norma greeted Frank at the door. I went back to the hotel and went to bed. Here's what happened while I was sound asleep...

Frank and Norma shared a few more drinks. Then Frank told her that he had decided, while at Tonopah, to return to his wife. That was the one thing she had told him never to do.

"What the fuck?" she said. "You beat on me all night long, then tell me you planned all along to return to your fucking wife?"

"She loves me."

"I love you."

"She ain't a whore."

Norma attacked him. He pushed her away. She grabbed a pistol from the nightstand drawer and shot him twice. He wrestled the gun from her.

She grabbed another pistol from the shelf and was about to fire again when Frank shot her through the heart. She died before she hit the floor.

Frank ran out onto the street screaming, "Me and Norma killed each other!" The policeman ran up to him. "I want to confess to murdering a whore."

The two men went inside. Frank hid the murder weapon while the policeman examined the body.

Frank was hauled off to jail. He changed his mind about confessing when he realized that his wounds were superficial.

A mob formed outside the jail. The next morning, Frank was escorted – for his safety -- back to Tonopah.

Without Norma, Amargosa wasn't fun anymore and I was getting tired of the smell of Borax. It was time to return to Texas to get that buzz cut.

Gone Fishing

Every day the little girl would stop by the graveyard, give me a sip of water from her canteen and a little bread to eat. One time she brought some raw oysters. I gulped them down and could feel my dick getting hard underground. Too bad she didn't bring a shovel to dig me out… If I could just move my arms. But I couldn't. I was too weak. The ants and beetles continued to chew away at my face. The little girl said that made me look like the Pal-Mal Man.

"I've heard that one before," I whispered.

I kept having these damn murder dreams… I kept seeing all their faces… Charlie's, Sadie's, Katie's, and Lulu's.

One day the girl brought a pair of scissors. She gave me a haircut and trimmed my beard. While she was doing that, I watched as this white man in a black hat rode up. I thought I was back in the dream.

The man got off his horse and dug me out.

"Thank you and you're under arrest for the murder of a bunch of rich people."

"How did you know about that?"

"I'll ask the questions around here." But I couldn't think of any questions to ask him. I handed the man's gun to the girl. "Little Lil," I called her, "take this man back to Los Angeles to stand trial."

"Where are you going to be, Assman?"

"I said, I'll ask the questions around here. Consider yourself deputized."

"But I'm only four years old."

"That's old enough. Besides, girls mature faster than boys. You're eighteen in terms of man years... You're eighteen in terms of man years... seventy-nine compared to the Acting President."

The bad man laughed.

"Such a brave little girl," I said. I mounted her on the horse behind the bad man and cocked the revolver. "Keep the gun pointed on his back and pull the trigger if he tries anything funny."

"No!" cried the murderer.

"Shut up, you. And thanks again, for saving me."

"Don't mention it again, Assman."

"Okay, I won't... Don't call me, Assman."

"Shouldn't you cuff his hands to the saddle horn?"

"Oh, good idea, Lil."

"Hey, man!"

"Shut up, you!"

"But I—"

"I said shut up! And get a haircut, you hippie bas-turd."
... I tied his hands well and tight, then slapped the beast on
the flank before it could kick me in the balls. "Yah!"

I watched them gallop off.

I found my horse. That was the good news. Well, it
wasn't my horse. It was Johnny Behen's horse. But it was my
horse now.

...Devil's Hole is one of the Wonders of the West, if not
of the world -- a geothermal, pussy-shaped pool on its surface
that is found within a limestone cavern in the Amargosa
Desert. They say that when there's an earthquake in Chile or
the Far East, the water level of Devil's Hole rises four feet.
Devil's Hole pupfish are found nowhere else in the world.

I spotted Johnny Behen there fishing... He had built a fire and was frying up a mess of pupfish... I investigated the spring and didn't see any more fish swimming around.

"Didn't you see the sign?"

"Sign?"

"No fishing. I'm afraid I'll have to cite you."

"Fine. Then I'll arrest you for the murder of P.G. Pimperton."

I tore up the citation. "We square?" No response. "I said, 'Are we fucking square?'"

His pole bent hard, and I don't mean his dick.

"Fuck! I got another one. This one's a big motherfuka."

He fought it for a while during which time he told me all about the plane crash and how he had just been released from the lunatic asylum in Waco and had come out here to find Lizzie Bordone, apprehend the man behind the Fergoosen killing, and, most importantly, charge Lecher Christian with assault."

Behen pulled on the line and a diver popped out of the water and onto the bank. I drew my gun as the man took off his helmet. I recognized him as Mike Nelson, the silent porno star.

"I ain't no habeas corpse," he said, He looked at the fish frying over the fire."

"I'm afraid I'll have to place you under arrest, Mr..."

"Behen!"

"We've been all through that," I said. "Consider it handled." He gave me a puzzled look. "Brandon Assman, federal under-the-covers investigator..." I searched my pockets. "My identification must be dead and buried."

"You want me to throw the bones back in?" Behen asked.

"Just don't do any more fishing at Devil's Hole," Mike warned. "Any other divers rise to the surface?"

"None since I've been here," Behen said.

"Fuck! There are all sorts of caverns down there...I might have to teach you boys deep-water diving."

"How far down you get?" I asked.

"1,200 feet and couldn't descend any further."

"Damn... Hungry?" Behen asked.

Mike licked his lips. "What you got?"

"Pupfish."

He sat down. "What the hell... They're only the world's rarest fish. The only species that can thrive in the oxygen-poor, ninety-one-degree water." He grabbed a piece off the grill and bit into it. "Not bad."

"You bring any lady silent porno stars along with you, Mike?" Behen asked. "Like that Veronica? She's hot."

"It's so fucking beautiful down there," Mike mused, looking at the spring."

"I'd like to get my nose up in her."

THE WITCHES OF TEENOGRAPHY

How can I describe my time among the lesbian dick-takers -- learning the secrets of Teenography as cribbed from the University of California's medical records by Don Juan Castaneda – except by telling it?

As Furtha Ada0-Do would say, "It's complicated." And I was flying on mescaline at the time.

… Traveling by horseback through Death Valley – the hottest, driest, lowest place on earth during this time of year – while being eaten alive by giant insects during the summer is like being on a bad acid trip.

The stifling heat, rising in waves from the chalky desert floor, bore down upon me. There was no wind. No sounds at all. Only stillness. And no shade anywhere. The desert was unrelenting. I took a last sip from my canteen which I had filled at Devil's Hole four days ago. I had gone from the graveyard into the fire. If only I could find a pool or even a mirage somewhere to jump into. Maybe it was divine retribution for having dined on the endangered pupfish.

I dismounted at the base of a dune and lay down under Behen's horse to get out of the sun. Turning over, I noticed this cactus that looked like a big, green tomato except that it had pink flowers growing out of it... Peyote. Since I hadn't eaten since my illicit seafood dinner, I pulled out my knife, cut the plant from the sand, and then sliced it into pieces. I bit off a piece and started chewing. I almost threw up. It was like eating cream cheese that had set out in the sun for two weeks. Somehow, I managed to get the plant down me, fighting off a gag reflex the whole time. I noticed a few other peyote plants nearby, freed the cactus and stored them in in my saddlebag.

I mounted my horse and started up the dune. The psychoactive properties of what I had ingested were beginning to take effect.

Near the top of the dune, I spotted what seemed to be the entrance to a mine shaft. I dismounted and stepped past the wooden crossbeam entrance to get out of the sun. Thank God! I secured my horse in the portal, lit a match, and began working my way into the mine which turned out to be a maze of passageways, drifts, and adits. I had used up half my matches when I stumbled on a rock and went hurtling down a shaft, bouncing off a mattress and into the arms of a naked lady. I looked around. The cavern was more of a great hall with marble floors, high ceilings, cloth walls, and prehistoric artifacts scattered about with eight to nine-foot-high mummies along a wall.

Fortunately, the two ladies in the bed with me were not nine feet tall or I would have had a devil of a time fucking them…The beautiful, naked lady sandwiched between me and the other gal turned on her side like she wanted to go back to sleep. She was a brunette with a hot body and full, perky tits.

"Well, hello," I said cheerily. "And who might you be?"

She opened one eye. "Don Juan?"

"I don't mind if I do," I said, pulling out my dick and climbing on top of her.

"Hey! What about me?" said her companion.

I kissed the first one on the lips. "What did you say your name was, baby?"

"I'm not a baby. I'm a witch."

"That's Poison," said the other one. "I'm Quote Unquote. The baby is over there." I turned my head where she indicated to see a blonde, grown woman playing on the floor with dolls.

"She seems happy enough."

"You should know. You infantilized her," Poison said.

"When was that?"

"Before you died... You don't recognize me?"

"Should I"

"I'm the little girl, Lil who kept you alive in the graveyard."

"But I sent you off with the bad man who dug me up."

"Sorcerers can be in two places at one time," Quote Unquote explained.

"How is that possible?" I asked.

"Here. I'll show you." I could discern a body crawling under the covers.

"Well, thank you, Poison."

"Don't mention it..."

"Please excuse the mess." Quote Unquote said. "We're remodeling,"

"Come and find me," said the woman under the covers.

"Oh, you wanna play, huh?"

Poison held me in place. She was a lovely brunette with an animated face. I wanted desperately to fuck her… I mean, I wanted to fuck her desperately… Oh, I don't know what I mean… My head was so fucked up… But her twitchy face was a distraction.

I kissed her lips passionately to contain the silent movie show that was her face.

I'm a wicked witch, all things considered, but we've got some real bad-ass witches as I'm sure you know, Don Juan who are even worse than me."

"Like whom?"

"Like me." I looked up.

" This is eyebrow-raising."

"You can get Botox for that… Who are you?"

"Bad-ass witch," Poison whispered. I could feel something wet on my dick under the covers.

"Gobby Smack. You may have noticed that I'm insecure."

I stared into her mouth, past her tongue, down her throat, and into her soul…. She was a thin, haggard, spikey-haired, small-breasted woman with close-set, sunken eyeballs and a nasty streak about her. She looked like four or five different women uncomfortably pounded into one.

"You look like you need sleep."

"Am I all that unattractive?"

"I didn't say you were unattractive. I said it looked like you needed sleep. So get in the bed with us."

"… Well! And who are you?"

"What do you mean?"

"You ain't Don Juan Castaneda."

This lovely Black woman walked over. "But Gabby. Remember the others? You said they were all Don Juan dressed up like miners."

"But their dicks were different, Abby Fine."

"Don't remind me."

"Why don't we all just get under the covers?" I suggested. "Oh, that feels good."

"We learned our lesson with those guys. Don Juan is dead, dead, dead as God himself…I'm awaiting an answer," Gobby said.

She swore right through me… I mean, stared right through me, as though she could see into my guts.

From under the covers, Quote Unquiet's alter-ego's mouth on my dick felt good. "A rising dick raises all boats," I noted.

"That doesn't even make sense," Gobby asked. "I'm waiting for an answer."

"What is your trip, bitch? I find missing lambs and bring them home to--."

"No, you don't!" she said harshly, "Don't play us for stupid. We all have PhDs from the University of California except for Abby who has only got a Bachelorette's from Harvard."

"Don't remind me," Abby said with a shudder.

Abby didn't like being reminded of much.

"You're the Coward from Bitter Creek," Gobby continued. "Aren't you? … You also killed a man for no good reason, didn't you? … A Mr. P.G. Pimperton to be exact. Don't think you can fool us. Like I say–"

"I know. You all have STDs from Harvard or some damn place…. Damn, I'm coming!"

"University of California!" Gobby screamed. "Except for Abby who's the only one with a Bachelorette from Harvard."

"Don't remind her."

"Thank you," Abby sniffed. "I may be dumb but I'm beautiful inside and out."

"I'll do you," I promised.

"I'm married."

"So, you've been fucked once or twice. No big deal."

"Where's your valise?" Abby asked.

I stared at this beautiful, Black chick.

"I didn't bring a valise. But my horse is up in the portal if you wouldn't mind giving him water, feed, a bath, and a blowjob... There's peyote in my saddlebag for your trouble.

"No trouble at all. Be right back." Just like that, she was gone. Then, before anyone could say another word, she was back.

"All taken care of."

This smiling redhead came to the surface and nestled in my arms while Poison tried unsuccessfully to push her away.

"What's your name?"

"Linda."

"Linda what?"

"Kastabian."

Gobby stared at the peyote that Abby was holding. "Put those in the blender,"

A blunder? I wondered.

I found out what a blunder was. It's one of those new-fangled inventions where you throw in all this nasty shit you wouldn't dare to put in your mouth, mix it up into one big container of crapola. The plan was to demonstrate these benders at the St. Louis World's Fair. I don't know how these witches got-- well, I guess I do know how they got hold of one so fast. They're witches after all.

Abby poured smoothies for us all. Soon we were all naked on the big bed, holding each other's noses and gulping down this swill, except for Blue Scout, the blonde, who kept playing with her dolls.

"She's a born-again virgin," Poison explained. "I mean, pagan… I mean pagan/virgin."

"Sure," I replied. "Do you all sleep together?"

"It's either that or we all sleep separately," said Poison. That made sense to me in my diminished haze.

"What do you have." Gobby asked. "a million girlfriends?"

"Nooo… Only a couple hundred thousand… Let's see… There are six to eight of you all on the bed. That means two or three of you have got to be on your periods."

"Guess which ones," Poison said.

"Okay… You and (I had no idea, so I made a wild-ass guess) _ Abby."

"Guess again…"

I was getting tired of these guessing games and just wanted to fuck. But it wasn't that simple...

A new woman was in my face. "Hi! I'm Robite Tumbler and I know how to fly." She was an older woman, naked like the others. Her weathered skin indicated she had spent a lot of time in the sun. She forced her tongue into my mouth, then took it out and studied my own weather-beaten and ant-bitten face. "I'm all in for the poor garbagemen except when I'm banging CEOs. Are you a CEO?"

"Of course."

"Let's fuck."

"Wait... So, all you bitches are witches?"

"To one degree or another," Robite explained with a smile before jumping on my dick."

"She seems like a very impulsive lady," I explained to Quote Unquote.

"I hate her."

... I discovered that Mescaline and sex go together quite nicely. As the ladies and I became more intimately acquainted, I found myself looking steadily into the women's faces like I never had looked at anyone before. It was like I was seeing clearly for the first time and learning more about my witchy bedmates in the process.... I was beginning to care for them too, even though they were so much different and so much better than me, I was only a simple gumshoe after all, while they had all these advanced degrees --except for Abby who only had her bachelorettes from Harvard -- which indicated they were witches of the highest order, not like those sluts Macbeth fucked. Being high on mescaline like I was, I wanted to believe the best in people. I guess I've always been gullible which is why I'm such a lousy private eye. I would just like to spit on myself sometimes. Psst, psst!

Then I thought, what was I even doing out here in the desert? It didn't make sense. Suffering in this extreme heat, being eaten alive by prehistoric insects, dying of thirst, begging a bunch of lesbian witches for sex. Why should I care if some guy I didn't even know had been murdered or not? People get away with murder every day of every year. It's impossible to keep up with it all. So, why even try when I could be sleeping in a nice comfortable bed with a willing woman or laying on a Hawaiian beach like Samuel Clemons enjoying my wretched life as much as was humanly possible? It just didn't make sense. What did it all mean?

Quote Unquote's voice brought me back to my altered state of consciousness.

"We're so horny," she said, as though she could read my deranged mind.

"I'm not."

"That's because you're lesbian, Furtha Ada0-Do."

"That doesn't make me a bad person."

"Did I say it did?"

I guess the witches were beginning to feel more comfortable with me because they disrobed further and jostled to have me.

"I have a good feeling about this," Abby said.

"I'm enjoying a good feel too," I replied. "I deserve this after having been left for dead in the graveyard."

Linda was blowing me again.

"That's how to do it. Keep up the good work…. Don't forget about my horse, Gobby Smack. We both need a lot of attention."

"You were dressed as a miner the last time we saw you."

"That wasn't me."

"What are you supposed to be this time?"

"A bum."

"We'll clean you up with our tongues, won't we girls?"

"That's right, Robite. We like girlie men like you," Furtha Ada0-Do said.

A statuesque (not nearly as tall as the mummies), stunning, magnetic, busty Polynesian witch entered the hall from one of the many passageways.

"I think I'll give you a new name," Gobby added. "Let me see... What should it be?"

"Pal-Mal Man?" I suggested.

"Exactly. Don Juan the Pal-Mal Man. Got one?"

"Got one what?"

"A Pal-Mal cigarette, silly"

"No, I already gave you the fruit."

"How rude. Ain't that rude, Blue Scout?"

"We don't scare easy," she replied before turning back to her dolls.

"Can't we all just get along for as long as I'm going to be here?"

"What makes you think you're leaving?" Gobby said ominously.

"I think we're getting along just fine," Robite said, sitting on my face.

"Glad you think so." I tried to say.

"Well, that's gratitude for you," Poison griped.

The Polynesian witch removed her clothes and joined the rest of us on the bed.

"What's your name?"

"Yaawa but Carlos renamed me Talia Bay."

"That's no good. I'm changing it back to Yaawa."

"Thank you! Hey, everybody. Pal-Mal Man changed my name."

"To what"

"Yaawa."

"I like that."

"Has a nice ring to it."

"You never told us what you're doing here," Gobby persisted.

"Tell us," Abby said gently.

"I can't. Not with Robite sitting on my face," I said in a muffled voice.

"Get off, Robite," Gobby insisted.

"Oh, my God! Your face is all bloody."

"So now we know." Abby used a wet rag to clean my face.

"You'll have to forgive, Robite. She recently returned to us after ten years of living in the future."

"I've done a little time traveling myself, which I'm sure you witches already know."

"We do."

"Why can't you be sweet like her?" I said to Gobby.

"Like whom?"

"Abby."

"Look. We're not as stupid as you think. We all have PhDs in Sociology from the University of California… You need discipline and we're going to give it to you… We're going to teach you the principles of Teenography."

And what, may I ask, in a nut hole, is Teenography."

"In a nut hole, it's the study of teenaged sexual movement in girls."

"Ah."

"Don't change the subject."

"Which is?"

"You."

"Come on, Daddy," Robite said. "Tell us the story of Bitter Creek."

"How did you know about that?"

"We're witches, remember?"

"They said I ran away."

"That's the worst thing a man can do."

"… While all the men under my command took shrapnel."

"And did you?

"No, I took LSD, is all."

"And you expect us, as intelligent and highly educated witches, to believe that?"

"Up to you."

"What was the real reason that you deserted."

"Because I have a sweet tooth."

"But why didn't you withdraw your men with you?"

"You know, you have very kissable lips, Abby," I said, kissing them.

"What would you do, Pal-Mal Man," Poison asked, "if you had it to do over again at Bitter Creek?"

"Never have been there in the first place. Who cares about Bitter Creek? It's so tiny that you can't even swim in it."

"What was the objective of the mission?"

"To push on to Rock Springs where we could get some Chinese crib pussy… You have very small titties, Gobby."

"So, by getting your men killed, you had all the pussy to yourself."

"Something like that."

"Very clever."

"Thank you."

"What's your excuse for murdering P.G. Pimperton?"

"That's easy. I wanted to marry his wife."

"And did you?"

"Yep."

"Good for you!"

"Thanks, again."

"And what do you mean, I have small titties? Put them in your mouth, Pal-Mal Man… That feels good. You do that better than Don Juan."

"Don Juan was bullshitting you."

"He trained us how to get in touch with our inner sluts," Quote Unquote said.

"He didn't train you very well."

"True," Gobby replied. "He said he would never die but did. We could have inherited millions, but we came out here to commit suicide instead."

"Why didn't you?

"We needed the money to remodel this place," Poison interjected.

"Blue Scout did commit suicide," Gobby reminded the ladies.... "At least, one of one of her did. The other is over there playing with dolls."

"One of me is escorting Pal-Mal Man's prisoner back to LA," Poison said.

"And don't fuck it up," I replied.

Blue Scout looked up from her play. "Don't think we don't know what's up because we do. Witches always know." She stood up to leave.

"What's wrong with her?"

"Who cares?" Gobby replied. "It's all about me, not her or anybody else. I don't want you seeing other women... Why is it so important for you to fuck our pussies, Pal Pal Man?"

"I don't know. It just is."

"How will you feel about it after?"

"Bad."

"Then there must be something more to life."

"It's enough for me."

"You're a man who's easily satisfied."

"I'd like to find Augie O'Henry too. But not as much as I'd like to fuck your pussies. It would mean a lot to me."

"It wouldn't mean much to us."

"That's sad."

"We'll fuck you if you like," said Quote Unquote.

"Okay, let's do it."

"So, we did. It was very nice while it lasted. But when it was over, I wanted to leave."

"I'd better check on Blue Scout," Abby said. "She's been gone a long time." Abby arose from the bed, walked further into the cavern, and came right back. "Blue Scout has fallen down a shaft! She's hanging by her fingernails. "

We all ran over to the shaft. I could see her down there.

I looked at the witches. Furtha Ado0-Do looked like the strongest one. "Hang on to my dick, Furtha, and lower me down." She did so.

"Lower… Lower… Suck on it… Make it longer." … I could…barely reach Blue Scout's fingers. "Oh, my God, that feels great, Furtha… Don't worry, Blue Scout. I got you… I did too. Until she slipped through my fingers and fell to the bottom of the shaft. Furtha pulled me back up and the two of us fucked some more.

"Damn, she's on her period." Poison said.

"Now we know," I replied.

"Did we have a bouncy bed at the bottom of that shaft, Poison?" Gobby asked.

"Uh… no."

Hot Air

I explained to Mary Ann how famous I was and suggested she fall in love with me. She said that she'd try... The old man, Ben, liked me, and his boys, Hoss and Joe wanted to fuck me. Joe was kind of cute and rode a Palamino horse that Mary Ann adored.

Mary Ann and I had a threesome with Joe's Palamino. Adam wasn't kidding about Mary Ann. She was a cutie. The Palamino wasn't bad either.

Mary Ann said she had tried to fuck Joe on numerous occasions but that he always turned it into a joke and had this high-pitched laugh like a girl. I asked Mary Ann to see if she could get the combination to the safe from Joe. She said that only Ben knew it.

So, one day, while Ben was unlocking the safe, I came up behind him and stuck my dick in his ass. That's how I got the combination. He also recommended a good Reno attorney who, he claimed, had a nice asshole.

The Ponderosa was lousy with queers. I stole one of the boys' horses and, with my saddlebags full and Mary Ann in tears, rode off.

Mary Ann was in love with me, alright. I suggested, in parting, that she find employment whoring in Virginia City and that I'd look her up next time I was down that way since I sure as hell wouldn't be welcomed back at the Ponderosa, except by the sheriff.

…. By the time I reached Reno, I was madder than a boiled lobster. The horse I stole had gone lame. I had to hoof it the rest of the way with the saddlebags slung over my shoulders. This was the second time that I had to crawl back to Reno…I looked all over town for Holly, but she was nowhere to be found.

After I completed my bank business, I found the attorney, Mortimer G. Shyster Esquire, who Ben had recommended. I instructed Shyster to sue everybody in sight… the fucking Wright Brothers, Lech Christian, and Brandon Assman for stealing my horse. It seemed to be too much for Shyster to comprehend. We almost came to blows in his office.

"I must inform you, Mr. Behen, that people get beat up, their horses stolen, and their planes crashed every day," he argued. "What's so special about you?"

"Shut up, you silver-haired, old idiot-fuck!" I said, livid with anger.

"Now just calm down and tell me what happened."

"You should already know!"

"How am I supposed to know if you don't tell me?"

"I'm famous. Read a newspaper!"

"I've never heard of you."

"You're so stupid that I ain't going to waste my breath."

He got down on his knees. "Please, Mr. Behen. I need the business to buy nose candy."

"You should lower your fees."

"Help me… to help you…"

"Okay," I replied, barely able to maintain my composure. "… Christian hit me over the head, stole my whore and the lucrative naval sex trafficking contract I was trying to steal from him… Assman stole my horse. I spent three weeks in rehab because the Wright Brothers didn't know how to fly an airplane… Savvy?"

"I think I'm beginning to get the picture."

"It's about time... Look, simpleton... Assman is an *introvert* and Christian is an *extrovert*, if that means anything to you."

"What does that make the Wright Brothers?"

"*Perverts*," I said, slamming the door on my foot as I sought to leave his office.

I walked over to the depot only to find there was no train to Las Vegas.

I lost it at that point. "What the fuck good is the railroad?" I screamed at the ticket masturbator. "It never goes anywhere people want to go. What do I have to do, take the stage? My hemorrhoids will be hanging out from here to Christmas!"

"Well, there's hot-air balloon service in Reno."

"Where would I find that?"

"On the other side of the Truckee. You can't miss it."

He meant, the Truckee River.... Hot air balloons? How quaint!

... I had never been north of the river in Reno before... I watched as this very attractive brunette was inflating her big balloons.

"You should start a tittie enlargement service."

She laughed.

"Won't it break like a condom when you're up in the air?"

"I wouldn't worry about it. Where do you want to go?"

"Well, I was headed straight to hell, but I'd go to Vegas with *you*."

"Good choice. Tomorrow morning, they're auctioning off town lots to celebrate the arrival of the railroad from the west."

"From the west… I'd heard about that. We'd better get started."

She looked up. "It's fully inflated."

"So is my dick. How much are you going to soak me for?"

"Four hundred and fifty dollars."

My gag reflex kicked in.

"Or you can buy me a lot in Vegas."

"Forget about it."

"I'll throw in some free pussy."

"Bend over."

It was a beautiful day for a balloon ride, and I was enjoying the view down below. I'd forgotten all about Liz.

"I see what you mean about flying. It's awesome!"

"This your first time?"

"No, I've fucked before this.".

The basket swung in the wind, and I almost fell out.

"Let me help you," she said, moving so close that our lips grazed. "I'm Katie Davy."

"Johnny Behen."

"Careful. Hold on to me."

"With pleasure." She was a ravishingly lovely woman who seemed more artistically expressive than happy. Her face registered her feelings expressively. She had a winning smile but that would fade as our conversation progressed.

She had a beautiful smile – that was her default persona -- but her smile would fade as our conversation progressed, By the time I finished what I could think of to say, she would look at me like I was crazy. Well, maybe I was.

I noticed several expressions of mild disapproval... no, disappointment toward me. It seemed that I was missing out on opportunities to please and impress her. I guess I don't understand women, especially this strong, independent woman. Maybe we just weren't compatible. She sure was beautiful though. She seemed to be a woman who needed constant positive reinforcement which I'm not inclined to give women.

I had my arm around her waist as we gazed down at the desert view. "Think about it," she said … We live our whole lives slithering around like snakes in the dust when we could be soaring like this."

I kissed her. She responded passionately. We made love right under the balloon. It was so romantic. For a moment. When we finished, her smile faded into that look of mild disapproval.

"Now you must buy me *two* Vegas lots," she said. Damn. Her meter was running. We needed to arrive soon before she gained a controlling interest in the town.

"After I build my casino, I'll give you a piece of the action."

"I want to manage it for you too."

Pushy bitch.

"I just marvel—"

"What?"

"What?" It was hard to hear up here with the wind blowing her hair in front of her mouth as she was speaking.

"You just marble? … Mumbled?"

"I marveled.?"

"Did you come too?"

"What?"

"Why did you marvel?"

"… I forget."

Senator A.W. Clark was regaling the crowd and dignitaries from the caboose platform aboard his private Pullman train after it had pulled into Las Vegas from California for the first time. The Las Vegas trading post was to be a stopping-off point between Clark's Arizona copper mine and the coast. The dignitaries gathered in the shadows behind the pugnacious senator. The auction was being set up a few blocks away.

"… I thank God for this great country, my copper mines, my San Pedro, Los Angeles, and Salt Lake Railroad, the Montana state legislature for accepting my bribes to be appointed to the U.S. Senate, Senator George Hurst of California, who's standing behind me today, for his unwavering friendship and support, the blue dog wing of the Democratic Potty for its allegiance to redneck principles, my second wife, Chanel… where the fuck is she? …My dog and, oh, my children… People say I robbed the cradle when I married Chanel… It ain't true. My first wife robbed me of every dime I had… Why don't they tell you how Chanel robbed the grave when she married me? …Hehe. …, my daughter, Roulette —what happened to her? She's shy, by the way… intro-perverted. I got so many kids I could start a baseball team…

"I used to put on aerial shows in Texas and Oklahoma," Katie explained with her head in the clouds.

"Well, I'll be a goddamned sonofabitch. How did that go?"

"Good. Except I crashed into the Mississippi River once and almost drowned… Some fishermen pulled me out unconscious."

"That was nice of them. Did you suck their cocks in gratitude?"

"No, in Austin."

"I'm getting high. What's that smell?"

"Well, to inflate the balloon, I burn a combination of straw, kindling, and dried horse shit. As the straw burns, it heats the air in the balloon, and, well, hot air rises."

"I didn't know that."

"The burner keeps the hot air trapped during transport which allows the balloon to remain aloft."

"Fancy that." … My head was spinning. As Katie was adjusting our course with the ropes, I noticed a little dot down below that represented a stagecoach.

"Look at those suckers," I laughed. "I'll bet their asses are sore."

"Probably the ladies are sitting on the men's dicks and deriving some pleasure from that."

"Well, when you have lemons, make lemonade," I replied. "How much further?"

"Not long."

"You make this trip often?"

"Oh, yes. It's one of my most popular routes."

"I'm not surprised with you being such a wanton."

"… Las Vegas is an oasis in the middle of the desert, you know."

"Does it have water?"

"Underground springs and a lake."

"I figure when we get there, I can pick up some prime lots cheap and build a whorehouse," I said.

"A whorehouse?"

"That's right."

"You could call it the Flamingo Whorehouse."

"I could, but I won't… "

"So, what are you going to call it?"

"The Flamingo Whorehouse, Hotel, and Casino."

"Can I run it?" she asked,

"… Furthermore," Senator Clark continued, I'm going to keep on ballin' whores as long as my wife and daughter keep their backs turned… Senator Hurst and I are proud to represent mining interests in the U.S. Senate. I worked my ass off to get where I am today and earned every dollar I ever made in my life. I deserve a little R&R now and then, right, Senator Hurst? …This United Verde copper mine of mine in Arizona is pulling in a chill $400,000 a month and this little Vegas trading post is going to keep that money flowing… I control the means of production and transportation and the cost of labor. Everyone wins, especially me. People laughed when I bought up this land in Las Vegas, but who's laughing now? I am. To the bank… I thank the good Lord for this water-rich desert oasis where what goes on, stays going on… Now I know you folks didn't show up to hear me speechify but for the auction of *twelve hundred prime lots* right here in downtown Las Vegas which may not look like much now but give it a hundred years and I'm sure y'all will be mighty pleased with your investment in this great city… No need for a stampede as every one of these lots is Grade A prime real estate …This here is a landmark day in the history of Las Vegas, of Nevada, and of the United States, writ large…"

…Meanwhile, up in the sky, a flock of Rubber-peckers punched holes in our balloon. It burst in mid-air, falling on top of the train, enveloping the senator and his entourage, and tipping the iron horse into shallow Lake Sarah…. Screams emanated from the sinking passenger coach. Lights flickered off and on. Women were dumped into the lake. (Men were too but who cares about them?)

I advised the women to remove their heavy dresses, petticoats, and bloomers -- in fact, all of their clothing, including their underwear -- to keep from drowning.

I splashed up to Mrs. Clark, helped her to remove her heavy garments, then instructed her to float on her back and breathe normally while I fucked her with my inflated cock. She took my sound advice.

Meantime, the athletic and unsinkable Katie reached shore and headed for the auction. People were running from there to the scene of the accident just as the auction was getting underway.

"We'll start the bidding on this fine property at five hundred dollars."

"I'll give you eleven cents for it," Katie countered.

"Eleven cents? Why the survey alone—"

"Okay, ten cents."

… Exhausted but exuberant, Katie was able to bid successfully on the lots I wanted before fainting dead away.

Mrs. Clark and her naked daughter, Roulette, grabbed hold of me as I heroically swam to safety without getting bitten by a catfish. I stuffed the two exhausted women into a waiting stagecoach, then ran to the registrar of the auction. I only had to pay nine hundred and thirty-four dollars out of what I stole from Ben Cartwright for the entire block of lots that Katie had won for me. Then I engaged a contractor to build me a whorehouse and casino on the property before jumping into the stagecoach just as it was heading southeast to Prescott.

TRIPLE VISION

I mentioned Katie's idea to Chanel of getting my dick hard during the stagecoach ride and her bouncing up and down on it. She wanted to try it and came so many times.

"This is even better than doing it on the train," she screamed. "Where are we going?"

"Prescott. You wanna try it, Roulette?"

"Prescott?"

"No, my dick."

"Is it all right, mother?"

"Now Roulette," I interrupted. "You're a big girl. You don't have to ask your mother about every little thing."

She loved it too and came even more times than did her mother. Then again, Roulette is a lot younger than her mother and has more come in her.

"That's enough, Roulette. My goodness, child, you'll wear out poor Mr. Behen's dick and I won't get any."

"No, she won't. It feels good in there."

"Who knows if he might have to rescue us from drowning again and we'll need something to hold onto."

"I might have to ride this motherfukin' stage more often," I surmised.

...I heard gunfire and looked out the window. "I don't think drowning is our problem this time, ladies unless it's in our blood... Faster driver!" I yelled out the window.

"I see them redskins," said the shotgun man.

"You can't call them redskins. It's politically incorrect," I replied.

"Okay... braves."

I couldn't argue with that because of the Boston Braves baseball team where they got a hatchet on their uniform which is okay for some reason.

My eye was still giving me trouble from when Andi accidentally (I think) poked it with her nipple. Now I have dust in it. When I opened both eyes, I saw triple out of one, so it looked like I had six to eight women in the coach with me. When I stuck my head out, it damn nearly got shot off, I was freaking out over how many hostiles were chasing us.

"I see everything three times," I said to the ladies. "Who hasn't been on my dick yet?"

"We both have," Chanel said.

"What about you other four?"

Mother and daughter just looked at each other.

"I pray we reach Prescott or wherever we're going before getting killed," one of the six women said.

"Not only that but I got the deeds to my lots that don't need to get stolen."

Then it started to snow just like it did in that silent movie, The Searchers where John Wayne goes after this little girl who's getting fucked by Indians while Jeff Hunter keeps acting like a damn ass-wiper for the whole movie and he marries this ugly redskin.

The snow turned into a blizzard just like in the movie. With my good eye, I could make out a carriage in the distance. "Follow that buggy!" I shouted at the driver.

"I can't see shit."

"Then neither can the Indians."

"You can't call them Indians," the driver said.

"Oh, fuck. Maybe they just don't exist at all. Maybe we don't either. We just think we do."

The buggy in the distance turned out to be an outhouse. We crashed into it and went flying. That's the last I remember before waking up in this bordello staring at six big titties.

"What are your names?" I asked them.

"I'm Mae."

"And your friends?"

"You're delirious. Rest now and you can play with all my titties later."

I heard Mae talking to Chanel and her daughter who were resting in separate beds.

"He got his eye poked out and sees everything three times," Chanel explained.

"Oh, I see."

A Black man came in with some soup.

"The six ladies and I would prefer to sleep in the same bed," I remarked. "You can sleep on the floor."

"Drink your soup," Mae suggested.

I kept my eye on the Black man. "Who the fuck are you?"

"Reverend Jeremiah."

"You didn't spit in this soup, did you?" I couldn't see anything like that in it.

The women all crawled into bed with me.

"That's better. What happened to the Indians?"

"What Indians?"

I sat up and looked out the window with my one good eye. It was bright and sunny outside. I got into some female flesh before I finished my soup.

When I awoke, Mae and the preacher were gone. Chanel and Roulette were coming through the door.

"We paid for the room."

"With what?".

"Daddy's money," Roulette said.

"Do all you ladies intend to get fucked?"

Mother and daughter looked at each other again.

"What's wrong with you, Behen? You on drugs or something?"

"No, back in Reno I got poked in the eye with a big tittie."

"You already said that… Well, you won't have to worry about that with Roulette. She's small."

Roulette blushed.

"I'm not, though… Did you know I was bred in Europe?" her mother asked.

"Gangbanged?"

"Yes. A.W. was cheating with me on his first wife. When he found another woman, he sent me to Europe to be bred in high society."

"Sounds kinky."

"It was."

"I didn't know Senator Clark was that well-bred, like I am, for instance."

"A.W. is a self-serving man. Unlike Hurst, he came from nothing."

"I'm sure he jerked off a lot in those mines."

I began disrobing. Roulette blushed again. Mrs. Clark didn't.

"How do you like your sex?" I asked.

"I like it just fine. Roulette has never done it before though."

"Except with Behen and Daddy," her shy stepdaughter replied.

"You lying bitch!"

"So, I'm a lying bitch now," Roulette replied… Okay, got it. "I've done it lots of times."

I don't know why I got mad. I wasn't even married to her then."

"You need to marry me, Roulette," I said, "so I can get my hands on your Daddy's money. I'm tired of working for a living."

"When did you ever start, gigolo?" Mrs. Clark asked.

"Keep it real, Behen. Do you want to fuck us or marry us?

"Whatever is the best way to get to your Daddy's loot, Roulette."

"What I want to do is make my husband proud of me by becoming the only kind of woman he understands."

"I'm afraid to ask what kind of woman that is."

"A whore."

"A monkey could throw a wrench into that process… What about you, honey? (I meant, Roulette.)

"I want to have wild-ass sex too."

"And why is that, may I ask?"

I want to make Daddy proud of me I can get into his will and afford to buy more dolls."

"More dolls. I see. Yes, of course. Girls like dolls for some reason.

"I also want you to get me preggy."

"My God, Roulette! I can't afford to support a child on the money I've stolen."

"Don't worry. Daddy's got money to throw away."

Mrs. Clark came up and pushed me down on the bed.

"Hey!"

"Why don't you quit talking and get to fucking?" she said, removing her apparel. Roulette did the same. "It's good exercise, you know, and you look like you could use it. We want to be fucked like the sluts we intend to be."

"But I'm only one man."

"We'll see how good of one." She grabbed my cock and yanked on it.

"Ouch!"

Then she crouched over me and damned if she didn't stuff the whole damn thing up inside of her. Roulette pulled up a chair and sat down to watch.

"Open your cunty for him, little step-momma," Roulette coached.

Mrs. Clark was barely five feet tall.

"Oh, fuck, that feels good," I said.

"He likes fucking you, step-momma."

"Of course, he does. I was bred in Europe. What happened was--"

"Step-momma, you've already told that story... How is it?"

"Alright, but somehow I don't feel like a slut yet." She looked right at me. "You must be doing something wrong."

"Why does it always have to be my fault?"

"Step-momma -- lay down on your back. Mrs. Clark followed her daughter's instructions."

"Now, Johnny, get between her legs."

"Like this?"...

"Get in closer."

"If I get in any closer, my dick will be back in her pussy."

"That's an idea," Roulette concluded, appreciating the irony of the situation.

I stuck it in.

"All the way, Johnny."

"Yeah, all the way, Johnny," step-momma said. "What's wrong with you?"

"How's that?"

"Feels better."

"Step-momma, spread your legs more… Oh, that's hot… Do you feel like a whore now?"

"A little bit," she admitted.

"You look like one," I observed.

"Shut up, you!"

"I thought you wanted to be one."

"Oh, that's right, I do."

"What do you mean, 'I do'? You're already married. This ain't Utah."

"Close to Utah."

"This ain't horseshoes."

"That looks hot," Roulette said. "How does it feel, step-momma?"

Her eyes were rolled back in her head like she was in la-la land."

"I think she's enjoying her organism."

"Orgasm."

"That's what I said."

I pulled out and Mrs. Clark squirted like Old Faithful."

"My God!" I noted.

"I'm just getting started."

She was too. She squirted pussy juice every time I pulled out my dick.

"My toggle-stick likes how your pussy keeps giving it a shower."

"Don't stop now. Stick it back in."

"Sure. No problem.... Starting to feel like a whore?"

"Getting there."

… Finally, it was Roulette's turn. She lay down on the bed and Mrs. Clark scooted over to the edge where she rested on one arm so that she could observe the process without throwing a monkey wrench into it.

For some reason, women love to watch people having sex. But, to me, it's like wishing for the hands of a clock to move. Have you ever tried that at school when you badly wanted out of the most boring class in the history of the world? I don't recommend it.

I felt a real sense of accomplishment as my dick fought its way into Roulette's cunt. She was tight as hell, though she had no breasts to speak of. I had to sneak peeks at her stepmother's for inspiration. "Quit looking at my titties, Behen," Mrs. Clark said sharply.

"I didn't mean to," I lied.

"Mind your business... How does that feel, Roulette?"

"Okay."

"It's good for me," I said.

"Shut up! Nobody cares about you. We're in charge here."

"Yes, ma'am."

"Besides, you're a broke-ass, two-bit rich-woman-fucking gigolo, so keep your mouth shut."

"Mother! Your good breeding."

"Yeah! How would you know how much I've stolen?"

"I thought I told you to shut the fuck up."

"You may have."

"Motherfuka always needs to score the last word."

"Bullshit."

"That better be your last retort, brat ... Now fuck her harder."

"Yes, ma'am."

"It wasn't," Roulette observed sadly. "If he got paid by the word, he'd be rich as Daddy."

"Just concentrate on your organisms, little lady."

"They're called orgasms, stepmother. For goodness' sake! You're so past the expiration date."

"They must not have taught her that in Europe."

"Shut up! … Lean over her."

"Are we making a silent porno?"

"Do as I say! …Rip her blouse… Lay on her… Now put your tongue in her mouth….Keep fucking her! Goddamn, he's slow-witted…"

"I wasn't bred in Europe, like you, ma'am."

"Drive it up in her."

Roulette screamed.

"… Like you mean it."

Roulette screamed again.

"Take it like a woman, Roulette… Show him those nice, little titties… So cute… Call her a fucking whore, Behen."

"But she's so sweet."

"I said, call her a fucking whore. Jesus Christ!"

"You fucking whore."

"Again, with feeling."

"You filthy, fucking whore!"

"Keep fucking her."

Roulette screamed again. "I'm coming! …. Oh, my God, I'm coming so hard!"

… I laid Mrs. Clark and Roulette side-by-side on their backs. First, I fucked Roulette. My dick felt good inside of her. Then I hopped over to Mrs. Clark and didn't waste any time getting my swollen member inside of her. I left both their drawers on them, the way the British do it, for added erotic effect. Then I went back and forth getting between their six-to-eight legs. I was kiss-fucking Roulette. I told Roulette how good it felt inside of her. She asked if I cared for her.

I could see Mrs. Clark getting jealous, so I went back inside her.

"You have such life on your fast cock. It vibrated so much inside me," Roulette explained. "I came so much. I'm still coming. She was rubbing her pussy. "I'm still coming without your help "

"I'll get royalties, right?"

"It feels so good. I'm so soft and wet inside. I love it!"

"Glad I could be of service."

I asked Mrs. Clark if she felt like a slut now.

"Not so much," she replied.

I couldn't hold back any longer and shot come deep inside Mrs. Clark's pussy."

"What about now?"

"To a certain extent."

"Goddamn, you're hard to please."

Roulette was still coming of her own volition.

I got up from the bed. My heart sank. Did my eye deceive me? I was hoping that it did because my brain was being told that four other women on the bed still needed balling.

"Now I want to see you and Roulette go at it together."

"I feel like you got the wrong woman preggy," Mrs. Clark said.

"With your money, you can always send it to a breeding school in Europe," I suggested.

BRANDI GOES TO WASHINGTON

Allegra went along for the sex. First, they met with the AARP to see if that group would be interested in supporting long-term care legislation for the elderly, the Civil War generation who had saved the union.

The Board said they had better things to do than help some wanton hookers get government handouts.

Then they went to see Ruly Drooliani, the Acting President's right-hand ball. That didn't go well either. They found Ruly in the White House residence shacked up with this little Negro girl, Victoria, who, Ruly said, was his cousin. Ruly got mad when the two grown cult members declined to join them in bed.

"Nothing personal," Brandi said. "I'm afraid you'd get all excited. We just don't like to have our fake titties drooled on, do we, Allegra?"

"Mine are bigger than hers,"

"I can see that. Do you think I'm blind?"

... A.W. Clark's dick shot straight up in his pants when the 56"-26"-45" Allegra with MM cups set foot in his office.

"Bring both feet in here."

Ruly said that he said he could be persuaded to support the cause if Allegra would allow him to fuck her ass while Brandi sucked his balls.

"It would be a little crowded under there, don't you think, Senator," Brandi responded, "with the four of us under you?"

Allegra, as patriotic as the next nympho, riffed into, "with liberty and justice for all…" Then she burst into song:

"God Blass America

Land that we love…

Stand beside her

And guide her

To the hay

In the barn

Where we lay."

"You would have a beautiful singing voice, Allegra if you'd give up the damn cancer sticks," Clark advised…. "A less raspy one anyway."

During Allegra's beautiful rendition of our nation's theme song, Brandi got all wet and creamy. But that was probably because Senator Hurst had his dick up in her as far as it would go.

… There was picketing outside the Senate hearing room, protesting Brandi's testimony before the Ways and Means Commitment which Hurst chaired.

Brandi had only appeared in two silent movies made the weekend she was in San Francisco Flirty Fucking on behalf of Father Sanders.

That didn't prevent the KKK from objecting to her appearance before the committee. "This woman does not reflect the white Judeo-Christian values of the KKK," Grand Dragon, Willard E. Freedom proclaimed.

"Why, she was gangbanging five, six, seven, eight, nine or ten (I lost count cuz I weren't too good at arithmetic) giant-dicked niggas! That there is in-constitutional," Freedom fumed.

They let the two lady religious leaders into the chamber anyway… Freedom was thrown in jail for disrupting a Senate hearing.

"Where's mah Roy Conehead?" fat Willard cried.

In her calm, sensible manner, Brandi testified about David Sanders who had received the Pink Heart during the war between the states for procuring so many hookers. "He has rescued so many House of David followers out of poverty, drugs, and hopelessness too.

"Recently, Father David, with all he must do managing us Flirty Fuckers, suffered a stroke after falling out of Gracie's bed. Now he has spit coming out his mouth and needs seven/eleven care, and have any of you gentlemen priced caregiving costs lately? Horrible."

"They don't even know the price of a slice of pizza these days," Allegra, sitting next to her, whispered.

"We simply cannot afford to pay these rising health care costs and Father may live for a long time yet."

Senator Hurst thanked her for devoting such heartfelt, thoughtful attention to this issue that none of the senators had heard about before.

Then Senator Clark stood up, lambasted the "feckless Ball administration" and offered a $50 reward, "because that's all it's worth to me," for information leading to the arrest and conviction of "whoever stole and is sex trafficking my wife and daughter," and "wouldn't it be nice if they could finally catch that escaped marathon motherfuka, Félix Uranus as well?"

Allegra asked Clark if he had any spare change for the train fare back to Waco. He said, no but check with Attorney General Reno because she was blowing up their compound there.

Believing that to be a bum steer, Brandi and Allegra went to a sign painter and had two colorful sandwich board signs painted that read, *Need Train Fare Home Will Fuck for a Dollar.*

They stole two tin cups out of the soup kitchen next door and made enough money in six hours to buy two train tickets back to Waco along with a pair of dildos so they wouldn't get lonely during the long trip.

After Willard E. Freedom was sentenced to ten years in prison, time-traveler, Roy Rutburn was named Acting Grand Dragon of the KKK. His pal, Vern Fronk was elected Secretary/Treasurer.

How this happened is anybody's guess. The thinking was that Roy was a hardline antisemite who would oppose U.S. intervention in the War in Israel or the Isreal/Hamus

Conflict, or That Middle East Bullshit, or whatever the press chose to call it that day. "It's wonderful," Hurst said. "I'm selling so many newspapers reprinting war news."

In any event, Roy's first order of business was to find some redneck pussy. He called Ruly Drooliani's office and made an appointment with the Acting President's alleged brain to get his advice.

… "I've never seen such big bazooms in my entire life," Ruly professed to Victoria. "With those balloons in her, it's a wonder that one doesn't float off into space," He was referring to Miss Allegra Kole.

Ruly's body man came in. and gave him a blowjob.

""That's enough for now. Kindly bring me whatever Victoria's having for breakfast."

"Eggs over easy with a hot beef injection," ordered the cute, little Black chick lying naked in the bed next to Ruly.

"You can administer the hot beef injections, Alfred."

"Very good, sir."

"Now get out."

"Yes, sir…. Oh, and there's two gentlemen here to see you."

"Throw them out. And who let those two low-life Christian whores in here," Ruly asked Victoria. "It was probably that goddamned Alfred… Government money for elder care," he said derisively. "Who ever heard of such a ridiculous idea before me? … Why, that money must be thrown away in the Middle East."

"Well, my mother—"

"Never mind your mother, she's Black… Such a silly idea, to give money to people who are about to die anyway. Their relatives would just steal it and then push Momma off the train. What do those bimbos think, the government is made of money?"

Victoria, who recently arrived in D.C. from Wyoming, looked critically at the decrepit old man shooting his mouth off beside her. "Couldn't the Treasury just print more? They are the Treasury, after all."

"Print more money? … I would expect an answer like that from one of your inferior race. Now get on this dick. It's all you're good for."

"I can cook and sew too."

"If I wanted a sewing lesson, I'd fuck Betsy Ross… What she did with the flag was treasonous. Whoever saw such an ugly flag before? … Now suck on this dick. It's getting hard again. No thanks to those fake-titted whores bursting in on us like that. Just about gave me a fucking heart attack."

"Rather than suck on your dick, how about, let's just talk? I love chatting with haters."

"I'll do the talking around here; you do the sucking. And I'm not a hater. I'm a lawyer making $350 an hour, for God's sake… Not with your hand! Put the whole goddamn thing in your mouth… Down your throat… Yeah, like that…"

Alfred came in carrying a tray. "Not now, Alfred. Can't you see I'm working? Get out."

"Very good, sir."

"He acts like a fucking butler, not a body man…You know, I was here the day that the British burned down the White House. What a day that was. I ran into the burning building and fucked Dolly Madison; I think her name was… Then I carried so many women and children out of the building. Not that many women, A few hot secretaries. I let the others burn… I don't know what ever happened to Dolly. I think she bakes cookies… Stay on that dick."

"I'm surprised you didn't catch cancer that day like so many other first responders did," Victoria gasped, "heroically saving all those women and children."

"A few men too. I wore a mask. What do you think, I'm some dumb wop? … Don't answer that."

"Don't forget to pay me."

"Pay you?" Ruly looked dumbfounded.

"You think I go around sucking honkey dick for free?" asked the young lady.

"Son-of-my-bitch! I'll have to write you a check."

Victoria looked dubious. "I don't usually take checks."

"Well, I don't usually pay Negro bitches for lousy blowjobs either. Now get out of here. Go pick some cotton."

Victoria went straight from the White House residence to the bank to cash the check that Ruly had given her. The teller informed her that the check was no good because there were only forty-seven cents in the account.

So, she left the bank and approached the first police officer she saw, appraising him of the situation.

"… Plus he made racially insensitive comments."

"You free or slave?" the officer inquired.

"Why, free, of course. My God!"

"Okay," he said, looking down at the check. "I'll investigate."

Officer Falstein didn't care much for Ruly when he was Mayor of D.C.

He liked him even less after catching up to him on the White House lawn... Falstein admonished Ruly about the check and about picking up common street prostitutes.

"Nothing common about that bitch. She sucks dick like a motherfuka," Ruly laughed.

Officer Falstein failed to see the humor.

"Then you should have paid her."

"Yeah, I stiffed her in more ways than one," Ruly chuckled this time.

"There's a law against kiting checks."

"There's a law against kikes serving as police officers too... Look, this was a nigga. She should have been grateful just to have some good dick and visit the White House for free. Negros, normally, are not allowed in at all, except through the black... I mean, back door where I brought her. So, you see, I've done nothing wrong. I even took a criminal off the street for a while."

Falstein didn't see it that way. "You want a medal?"

"No, I don't want a fucking medal. What I want is for you to go fuck yourself, Falstein."

"You're under arrest."

"Let's have trial by combat," Ruly screamed, and it was on.

The combat didn't go so well for Ruly, who was booked, fingerprinted, and tossed into the pokey with a couple of drunks and two Black guys.

Acting President Ball was furious when he saw Ruly's mugshot in the Post the next morning. "That fucker thinks *he's* Acting President.

"Bail is set at $500, Mr. President. You want me to pay the fine?" the president's body man asked.

"Fuck that. Let him raise the money the old-fashioned way, by taking it up the ass for a few days."

What Did You Do in the War, Daddy?

I had dismounted and was just finished rolling a joint when I heard a man groaning in the bushes. I decided to investigate. He had curly hair on the sides of his head but was bald on top. He also had a knife wound in his stomach. Said his name was Hughes.

"Howard Hughes?" I asked.

"Ronald."

I asked him if he'd had some sort of accident. He said, not exactly... that he was the attorney for Lulu in the Mansion trial but got scared and ran away and Clem, Dorn, Squeaky, and Brenda from the Family chased him into the rocks, stabbed him, and left him for dead.

"That's kind of like an accident," I said.

"How do you figure?"

"I use my fingers mostly. Sometimes I'll use the stick-in-the-dirt approach.

I lit the joint, took a hit, then handed it to him. He drew the locoweed deeply into his lungs.

"Well, I've got to get back to Los Angeles for the trial. If I don't, Lulu will fry for sure. She wants to take the rap for Mansion. I refuse to be a party to that and look what happened."

"What happened?"

"I got knifed and left for dead, man."

"Oh, that."

That was his story anyway and he seemed to be sticking to it. I had no reason to doubt the validity of what he was saying. But I couldn't prove it either.

We passed the joint back and forth.

The noon sun was straight overhead, and it was getting hotter than hell. I removed my white hat, wiped my brow, and took a long swallow from my canteen. Hughes licked his lips. "It's empty," I said.

"I've heard of Clem, Dorn, and met Squeaky. But who the fuck is this, Brenda?"

"Brenda Pitman. She's a bad one, man… Good-looking though. People tend to get killed or go missing when she's in the vicinity… Take me, for instance…

"Take you where?"

"Like I said, I need to get back to LA, man."

"Tell me more about this Brenda."

"She joined up with the Monfort gang after the Mansion killings…"

"The Monfort gang?"

"A White Supremacist, Aryian nations organization that robs drug dealers…"

"Sounds like they're a credit to their racist tendencies."

"They are that alright."

"What did you say your name was again?"

"Hughes… Ronald J."

"I never liked that name… Hughes."

It felt like the end of the line. After I had left Hughes, I headed straight for a lake that I could see clearly in the distance. The lake turned out to be no lake at all… I was lying in the desert, dying of thirst, slipping in and out of consciousness… I dreamed I was fucking the silent porno star, Veronica that Behen talked about. Or maybe it wasn't a dream. She turned out to be a real sweetheart. Punk face but a beautiful body. I didn't want to seem disrespectful, so I pulled out and came in her face.

…*A woman rode onto the rickety Rio Grande Gorge Bridge, dismounted, walked to the edge, and looked down. Below her, the gorge opened like a vagina with a stream of water running through it. A breeze arose that seemed to prompt the woman forward. Jan Emery extended her arms in front of her as if she expected to fly, and dove off the bridge, falling over five hundred feet to her death.*

"More shopping? You should watch your spending, honey." … *"Who the fuck are you? I'm saving with Liberty Bibberty, bitch. So, mind your own fucking business!"* … *"How dare you address your mother in that tone." "You ain't my mother. You're a pig!"* … That's strange… At least it's a different commercial, t thought… Then my show came back on…

There was a flash. Then an ear-splitting blast.

BOOM!

Then three more flashes in quick succession, quickly followed by three more blasts.

BOOM! … BOOM! … BOOM!

I was knocked senseless for what seemed like hours but may have only been a few minutes. I could smell gunpowder, shit, and vomit... I wasn't sure, but then the order of flashes and blasts seemed to shift, like baseball players running the bases back-ass-wards.

BOOM! ... FLASH! ... BOOM! ... FLASH! ...BOOM! ... FLASH!

Perhaps it was my mind that had shifted.

Staring dumbly into the haze, I perceived Corporal Outman running toward me... Outman was our Battalion's center fielder.

"Captain are you alright?" he asked anxiously.

"Not alright, Corporal," I replied. "What the fuck happened?"

"I don't rightly know, sir. It seems we've been attacked by Injuns and Rebs, both."

"Injuns and Rebs, both? Are you out of your mind, Outman? The way you play baseball, it seems like a linebacker playing center field... At least you knock the ball down half the time. Haha!"

"Yes, sir. Come quickly, sir. Major Patches has been hit."

I stood up and we raced through a hail of bullets. "Is he alright?"

"Not really, sir. There was a flash and then a blast…

BOOM!

… That knocked us off our feet. We got up and continued running to where the Major had fallen.

He appeared to be badly wounded. His pelvic region was torn up and bloodied.

"Are you alright, sir?" I asked.

"Not alright, Assman. It's bad. My dick's been shot off."

"That's going to make crib visitations problematical, sir," I frowned. "But you can always use your tongue and maybe get a discount."

"I ain't worried none about that. It's the Army I'm going to miss. The blood and gore of the Army. I love it so…"

"Steady, sir. You're delusional."

"The Army, Assman, is founded on the big pupfish/little pupfish concept…"

"Sir?"

"You know, the big pupfish eat the little pupfish…"

"I didn't know, sir."

"Yeah… In the Army, the captain gets to boss the sergeant… The sergeant bosses the corporal… So on and so forth…"

"I get to boss my privates," Outman said.

"Yes… You understand, Assman?"

"Brandon, sir."

"Assman! This is the Army, not one of your Parlor Houses!"

"No, sir. I mean, yes, sir… I'm a little mixed up, sir."

"Snap out of it, Assman! It's all up to you now. You're in charge. I tried to do my best. It's up to you to do the rest."

"I won't let you down, sir."

"I'm sure you will, Assman…. So, let me give you a piece of Army advice that applies to everything you'll ever do in life."

"What's that, sir?" The Major looked to be fading away…

"Wherever you go for the rest of your life, you must prove… you're a man."

"Yes, sir."

"And let me give you another piece of advice…"

"Not another piece of advice, sir."

"Just one more, Assman."

"Okay, one more, sir."

"Whatever you decide is the best course of action in any given situation, do the opposite."

"The opposite, sir?" Outman and I looked at each other.

"*I wouldn't give that advice to everybody, but you're different.*"

"*Yes, sir.*"

"*Now go and lead our troops to a glorious victory!*"

"*I will, sir!*'

"*Assman, I'm depending on you, son. To pull the company through...Assman, it's all left up to you...*

"*I've got this, sir.*"

"*That's what I'm afraid of... I'm depending on you, Assman. I've tried to do my best... It's up to you to do the rest.*"

"*I understand, sir.*"

"*Do you? ... Assman, I'm depending on you, son. To pull the company through. My son, it's all left up to you.*" *And then he was gone.*

"*What shall we do, sir?*" *Outman asked me.*

I remembered what the Major had just told me. I knew what I wanted to do... But I had to consider what was best for the company writ large. "*Attack, Corporal! Order an immediate attack upon hostile forces.*"

"*You've got it, sir! ... Listen up, motherfukas... Captain's orders. We're goin' in... Read... Set...Charge!*"

"*Oh, and Outman...*"

"Yes, sir?" he asked, turning back.

"In the future, try to take better routes to the baseball. You won't look like such a damn fool when the ball bounces off your head."

"Yes, sir… Where will you be, sir?"

"Protecting our rear flank."

"Very good, sir… Charge, men. Charge!"

Outman was immediately shot down like a dog.

I watched the other men move out and heard them yelling as they forged into Bitter Creek. I turned and ran in the opposite direction and didn't stop running until I reached the Joss House in Rock Springs. I jumped into bed with this half-bred, fun-sized little number named, Sarah Winnemucca… After our bodies fused, she told me a bedtime story about giants that had once inhabited Death Valley. She claimed the giants, who were originally from San Francisco, were cannibals who were eating her people, just not in the way I had eaten her… Her tribe, the Paiutes, declared war on the giants and killed most of them. The rest fled into a cave… The Paiutes stuffed the entrance to the cave with brush and mesquite trees, then set it all on fire. According to Sarah, the last of the giants died in the fire, which would explain the mummies that I saw in the witches' cavern… I pondered this before falling into a dream.

Lizzie Bordone was prancing merrily through the desert at the Barker ranch when she came upon me lying in the sand having a fever dream.

"You have legal experts? ... I'll give you legal experts," I said *grabbing my crotch. Well, okay. Give me legal experts for $40, Alex."*

Liz squatted down and pissed in my face.

"... Hey! What 'cha doin'? I was dreaming that I was on a Hollywood game show... that I was the star of the Hollywood game show. Then you came along and pissed in my face... like an animal."

"That last part wasn't no dream."

"I can't help but feel that I'm damaged in some way."

"That's okay. Do you mind if I stay here and watch you die?"

"Yes."

So, she went away.

"Wait! I didn't mean it that way." But she was already gone, like all the others.

I knew in my heart that nobody good would ever come along again.

… After a while, this other witchy woman showed up… It was that goddamn, two-faced Robite from the witches' protection program – the last person on earth that I needed to be with right now.

"Well, if it ain't the no-good, Wicked Witch of the West."

"That's no way to talk to your wife."

"My wife now, is it?"

"Wife, lover. It's all the same thing."

"Right. Okay, then… Something is wrong with me."

"There's absol-pollutely nothing wrong with you that a good blowjob can't cure." Robite was an incurable optimist.

She gave me one and it didn't help. I still felt lousy. "How about a cup of water?"

"A cup of water? You sure do expect a lot from your woman." With that, she disappeared.

Well, that's it. I'm fucked… Then I saw some sort of mirage on the horizon… As it came closer, I could make out three women… I settled back into my visions…

"… Name a famous poem by Sir Alfred Lord Tennyson."

"Uh… Is it… Crossing the Bar, Alex?"

"That's correct for $50."

"Oh, my God, I finally won something! … "

"Please select a new category…"

"Clowns for $100."

"I am a famous clown with a big, red nose and a red lipstick smile who likes to play with little girls. Who am I?"

"Uh… Johnny Behen?"

"… No, I'm sorry. The correct answer is Rusty Nails… You lose your money."

"Fuck!"

… The three women approached me. "Are you witches too?"

"I should say not! I'm Penelope Hurst, this is Miss Goodbody who recently time-traveled in from the twenty-first century…"

"I used to do that too. But don't much anymore."

"… And this other lady is Miss Emily Showers. We all recently escaped from the lunatic asylum in Waco."

"Showers? As in me and her should take a shower together?"

"No," Miss Showers said firmly. "As in, I'm going to kill your motherfukin' ass, Assman for murdering my brother,

Cobb Showers." She pulled out a pistol and aimed it at my stomach.

"Is that absol-pollutely necessary, Miss Showers? Perhaps we can work something out."

"What did you have in mind, Assman?"

"Brandon."

"Fine. What did you have in mind... Brandon? ... Oh, how I despise the very sound of that name."

"Well, how about I fuck you in exchange for you letting me be? How does that sound, Miss Showers? I'm dying here in this sun, anyway."

"Let me talk it over with my friends...." They commiserated for a moment. "No, that won't do at all." Fortunately, the sun was in her eyes and the instant before she fired, I flipped over onto my stomach and took the bullet in the ass."

"Come ladies," Mrs. Hurst said. "We don't want to be late for tea." They left me bleeding in the sand... Funny. I had forgotten all about having killed Cobb Showers. He had it coming... They all do... His sister was hot though.... I'd do her.

Just as I was about to pass out from either dehydration, heat stroke, or loss of blood, a little girl, the one who had rescued me from the graveyard, reappeared with Linda Kastabian.

"Hi, Pal-Mal Man," Linda beamed."

"I'm glad to see you two. Did you take the bad man to jail like I told you to do?" I asked Lil.

"He got away."

"Fuck. I swear to God… if you want anything done right in this world, you've got to do it yourself."

"What's wrong with you this time?"

"I got shot in the ass."

"Well, they say, out here, if the heat doesn't get you, getting shot in the ass will."

"You've got to help me. You're my last hope before I turn into an archaeological relic."

"Let's make love first."

"Are you crazy?... Linda might snitch… Look, if we're going to be doing that, you've got to first change back into the wicked witch, Poison Penis-Envie because I ain't going down just because you've got daddy issues."

TRUE DETECTIVE

"Charlie had Augie O'Henry killed," the ubiquitous Squeaky explained. "We should kill Acting President Ball."

"Whatever happened to Sadie?" I asked.

"She's locked up," Squeaky said,

"Like you should be."

"... But they let her out to turn tricks... She brought gonorrhea back into the hoosegow. Now all the guards have it." She laughed.... "He's coming around, finally." Squeaky was referring to me.

... I'd been laying up with The Family -- what was left of it -- at Barker Ranch in Golar Wash. I don't know how long... Charlie had been arrested that morning. Tex -- the Man in the Black Hat -- was also in custody having been recaptured in San Pedro trying to catch a steamer to God only knows where.

I was laying up alright, zonked out in Poison's arms, sucking on her nipple and rubbing her clit while recovering from my near-death experience in the desert.

Poison kept feeding me wine grapes while I played with her. Some other killers or wanna-be killers were there -- Sandi, Slim, Bruce, Cappy, and Gypsy. Linda, who I knew from the witches' coven, kept identity-shifting with Piggy. "I'm just here for the sex," Linda smiled, before transforming back into Piggy.

I rubbed my eyes which seemed to be deceiving me... Then they were both standing there together – the smiling redhead and the demure Mexican girl... I decided to worry about it later.

Lizzie looked horny and jealous of Poison. I think she wanted her tittie sucked on too. She missed her chance in the desert.

Lizzie had agreed to turn state's evidence against her boyfriend, Bobby, the silent porno star, in the Hitman torture/murder case. A bunch of others – just about half the Family -- were in custody too.

Squeaky, Cappy, and Lizzie were among the free ones who would show up outside the Hall of Justice every day of the trial to work on their kitting. Cappy just missed killing her grandmother. On her way to do the deed, her horse threw a shoe. She regretted having let Charlie down ever since. Cappy wanted to go when the killers left the ranch, but Piggy, who was driving, said there was no room in the carriage. Cappy said she felt frustrated that she hadn't gotten to kill a pig yet. Piggy, who had been eating her way out of the lightweight division. copped a plea and evaded responsibility for any of the murders.

"Whaddya mean, Charlie had Augie O'Henry killed?" I slurred.

"Don't try to talk, honey," Poison said, stuffing another grape in my mouth.

"Put this in his mouth too," Lizzie said. "For the pain."

I started sucking on a tab of something. It seemed that I had been tripping ever since I left Reno. I guess, for the most part, I had.

"… That was when we were living at the Warren Spahn Ranch," Paul explained. Augie was trafficking all these girls and reneged on a deal with Charlie, who didn't like the fact that Augie was balling Black women. Charlie thinks blackie is only on earth to serve white people and that Black men should not be allowed to breed white women… except for Charlie."

What was he saying? … Warren Spahn Ranch? Images of a hellacious curveball flashed through my mind.

Paul looked over at Slim and Bruce who were giving him cold stares.

"Then what happened?" I asked. "… Come on. We're just rapping, man. It won't go any further than right here.

"… Well, these guys loaded old Augie into the wagon…"

"What guys?"

"Tim and Bruce here," Lizzie said. "That's what Mary told me." Paul looked very uncomfortable. Lizzie was buzzed and didn't give a fuck. She just wanted to get in good with me, I suppose, because she was jealous of Poison's attentions. Lizzie knew she could have had me in the desert, ant-bit face and all. But now Poison wasn't giving me up… Or maybe… I don't know why she would talk like that. Maybe those two thugs had raped her, and she wanted to get even… Slim gave Lizzie one of those two-faced, bipolar looks that Charlie had taught them.

Feelings of nausea came over me that I can only describe as a hatred for that ass-wiper, Slim. All the men tried to imitate Charlie… I don't know what was in that tab, but I felt an adrenaline rush through my body like I was coming back to life. I wasn't afraid of these killers anymore.

I stood up and so did Slim. "Do that again, motherfuka."

"Do what again, Assman?"

"You'd better refer to me as Brandon from now on. There it was again --the smile that quickly morphed into a ghoul's grin. Like he was getting ready to take me on.

What Slim failed to see were the white knuckles forming on my fist. I swung, connected with his mouth, and his teeth went flying like bowling pins. Just like that.

"No need to thank me for the extractions." Blood poured out of his mouth. "Sit back down unless you want some more." I guess he didn't because he sat right down.

"Now... what's my name?"

"Assman." I knew I had to finish him fast before they all ganged up on me.... I kicked him in the mouth with the toe of my boot. The rest of his teeth flew out of his mouth. He started to crawl out of the room. "Where do you think you're going, bitch?" My body was on fire. I didn't stop kicking him until he quit moving,

That's how you gain the respect of killers. I sat back down. Everybody was staring at me. "Go on, Lizzie."

She shrugged her shoulders like she just didn't care. "There goes my date for the night... All these guys here plus Tex and some others dragged Augie down the hill behind the house, knifing him along the way until they got to the bottom of the hill where they left him for dead. Clem came back the next day with lime to pour over the body, but the body was gone."

"Maybe a big Turley Bird dragged it off."

"Maybe."

"That's a lie!" Bruce Dorn said. "They ain't no thing as a Turley bird like the one dragged Bob Turley off."

"You ain't makin' no sense, Dorn, I said, walking over to him… "I'm used to dealing with PhD witches like I met in the cave, not dumbasses like you."

"How well do you know them witches?" he asked.

"Pretty well, man." Poison and Linda laughed.

What's my name, Dorn?"

"Brandon, Godfather.

"Don't ever forget it. Now go turn yourself into the sheriff like Linda here turned herself into Piggy before I jam my boot up your ass."

"Yes, Godfather."

"I loved Charlie so much!" Squeaky mused wistfully.

"You loved everybody. Don't put it all on Charley," Slim said after popping his head up. I kicked it back down.

Dorn left and the women formed a circle around me. The ladies rotated clockwise with every one of them bending down in turn to kiss my dick. Squeaky put it in her mouth.

It's always nice to collect a reward for solving a murder or two.

ABOUT THE AUTHOR

Purvis Carver was raised in Sulpher Springs, North Carolina with his father, mother, three brothers, sister, grandpappy, grandmommy and great grandmommy, uncle, aunt, dogs, cats, chickens, and a skunk come up from the river and live under the house.